B E S T
WOMEN'S
EROTICA
03

BEST
WOMEN'S
EROTICA
03

Edited by

Marcy Sheiner

CLEIS
PRESS

Published in the United States by Cleis Press Inc., P.O. Box 14684, San Francisco, California 94114.
Printed in the United States.
Cover design: Scott Idleman
Text design: Frank Wiedemann
Logo art: Juana Alicia
First Edition.
10 9 8 7 6 5 4 3 2 1

Excerpt from *Portrait in Sepia* by Isabel Allende appears courtesy of HarperCollins, New York, NY, 2001. "Strawberry Surprise" by Clio Knight was originally published in the July 2001 issue of *Australian Women's Forum*. "Envy" by Eden Lenz was originally published in the fall 2001 issue of *Mind Caviar*. "Man and Woman: A Study in Black and White" by Rachel Resnick was originally published in *Best Fetish Erotica*, edited by Cara Bruce (Cleis Press, 2002). "The Trouble with Claws" by Jean Roberta was originally published on www.suspectthoughts.com. "Bad Girl" by Alison Tyler was originally published in *Guilty Pleasures*, edited by M. Christian (Black Books, 2002). "What You're In For" by Zonna was originally published in *Tough Girls*, edited by Lori Selke (Black Books, 2002).

Acknowledgments

Personally, I am extremely grateful to Felice Newman, Frédérique Delacoste, and Don Weise, all of whom have been wonderfully supportive during what has been a difficult year for me.

Politically, Cleis and the other brave independent presses that provide a forum to explore sexuality through the written word, deserve a round of applause. I'd especially like to mention Bill Brent and Black Books.

For J.F. and all the sex-crazed ghosts
in the basement

TABLE OF CONTENTS

ix Introduction: Girls Just Wanna Have Fun   *Marcy Sheiner*

 1 Betty   *Ann Dulaney*

16 Strawberry Surprise   *Clio Knight*

21 Cat and Mouse   *Betty Blue*

27 Bad Girl   *Alison Tyler*

31 London Derrière   *Dawn O'Hara*

46 Red Lace Teddy   *Celia O'Toole*

51 The Trouble with Claws   *Jean Roberta*

60 Thought So   *Cecilia Tan*

67 Man and Woman: A Study in Black and White   *Rachel Resnick*

85 Memories   *Barbara Roduner*

95 Saturday   *Marcy Sheiner*

103 Too Bad   *Cara Bruce*

116 Mail-Order Bride   *Saira Ramasastry*

127 Kamini's Story   *Cheyenne Blue*

141 Envy   *Eden Lenz*

152 Plain Women   *Lisa Prosimo*

160 Lap Dance Lust   *Rachel Kramer Bussel*

165 The Price She Pays   *Michelle Scalise*

173 What You're In For   *Zonna*

187 Excerpt from *Portrait in Sepia*   *Isabel Allende*

196 Am I Naked Yet?   *Jane Underwood*

199 About the Authors

205 About the Editor

Introduction:
Girls Just Wanna Have Fun
Marcy Sheiner

Erotica can be many things: titillating, satisfying, profound, silly, wild, sweet, sad, funny, hot. One thing it usually is *not*, however, is boring. The stories in this fourth edition of *Best Women's Erotica*, as well as the characters who inhabit them, vary widely. There's the exuberant cook in "Strawberry Surprise," who laughs and lolls her way through the kitchen, gathering whipped cream, berries and semen to her naked body. The women in "Lap Dance Lust" and "Cat and Mouse" seek out fun by casually entering what was once a boys-only club: the world of sexual entertainment. And the dildo-wielding gal with the big ass fucks her musician boyfriend as a performance encore—and shows him which end is up.

Of course, not all sex or love or life is a barrel of laughs. Some of the stories have a sad, wistful quality, a sense of broken lives and broken dreams. Take Betty, the eponymous woman of the opening story. Betty might have marched straight out of Larry McMurtry's wide Texan landscape, with her sighing resignation to life's disappointments, her acceptance of her own limitations. Or Kamini ("Kamini's Story"), whose fate, for better or worse, is determined by ancient cultural traditions. Or Aurora, the character in Isabel Allende's recent novel, *Portrait in Sepia*, who stoically endures a loveless marriage to maintain familial harmony.

I particularly admire women who, though fun is far removed from their circumstances, relentlessly sniff it out. Silidi, the "Mail-Order Bride" from Sri Lanka, is so desperate to get to a place where she can find pleasure that she latches onto a complete loser who has just one saving grace—he's American. Silidi's fun quotient shoots off the charts when she utters those two little words—"I do"—in exchange for a green card.

The teenage shoplifter in "Saturday" has her own transgressive idea of fun. By the way, this is my story, so while we're on the subject, I feel compelled to note that it was not *I* who chose to include it as a "Best of..." Rather, my publisher, Felice Newman, strapped me to a chair and held a loaded gun to my head while she raided my computer.

The racial dynamics in "A Man and a Woman: A Study in Black and White" might not come as a surprise to American readers—but *will* provoke some thinking; then again, the racial elements may just melt into the background while the heat generated in the writing allows the body to take over. Similarly, readers won't need a Freudian interpreter to understand how the teenage girl in "Memories" might grow up to be the woman in "Bad Girl," or how the bad girl might evolve into the prostitute in "The Trouble with Claws." That is, if the fire generated by these stories doesn't stop all the noise rattling around our heads.

And isn't that one of the reasons we love sex? It shuts down the noise in our heads so that our bodies can go on a pleasure trip. In the end, it's really that simple; girls *do* "just wanna have fun." I for one am grateful for pornography, especially this particular genre—women's erotica, selected with fun-loving girls in mind. When there's no available or suitable partner—or even if we just feel like doin' it for ourselves—we can open up a book filled with vibrant characters and vivid sexual imagery, confident that eventually someone is going to fuck and/or suck, and take us along for the ride.

Unlike the confused narrator in "Too Bad," who seeks out "dangerous" lovers as a quick route to adventure, you, dear reader, can embark on *this* adventure right in the safety of your own cozy beds.

Marcy Sheiner
October 2002

Betty

Ann Dulaney

Betty's not the name she was born with, but it's served her well enough.

When you think of the name Betty, you think of a flour-dusted housewife wearing Avon cosmetics and bearing French's green-bean casserole to a block party potluck. You think of a bee-hived waitress in a diner that serves blue plate meatloaf and mashed potatoes to a clientele willing to plunk down two dollars and forty-nine cents in assorted change for it. You think of a member of a Gals'-Nite-Out bowling team, the kind that wears matching starched turquoise shirts that say "Bluebelles" in broad cursive across their backs. You think of a kind of dessert, or a cartoon character.

Betty is none of those things, yet in a manner of speaking she is all of those things too.

When you first see Betty, like Billy did that June evening, all you want is for her to love you back. As Betty knows perfectly well, that's pretty much all anyone needs, to be loved. When you're with her, you feel like you don't want to be anywhere else.

Betty washes her hair and sets it in rollers in the late after-noon when her day is getting started; she lets it dry out on her fire escape while she sips Folgers Instant from a brown mug. Her bedroom faces east, and the fire escape is done with its share of sun by the time Betty comes to stretch out her legs. Her eyes are retro blue, the color of an open '57 Chevrolet with fins the size of surfboards and a back seat wide enough for six or seven good-looking greasers plus herself. Betty's eyes are just that blue.

Betty's hair is her pride and joy. True, you could say she spends a little too much time at the sink with her head under the chugging faucet. The neighbors have been known to com-plain. It's a kind of escape when the Texas sun is making the broken glass in the street twinkle like the stars above, and the stars in the night sky are too dim what with the dust on the road. It helps to drown it all out with cool rust and minerals and a deprived sense of hearing. It's a transition from bed to being. Betty lets it rain down over her head, rinses out her hair real good, rinses all the aftershaves, the colognes, and the other man-smells off herself--and gets ready to start all over again. Watching the water collect where her bottle-blonde curls have stopped up the drain makes her forget who she is, and she'll stay there longer than you'd think a person should.

Ever done that yourself? Try it sometime. It's a lot like hanging your head over the side of a dock on a spring after-noon. You lie down on your back, tip your head over the side and let all the blood collect in your brain. It doesn't take but a minute before the sky becomes the lake, and the lake becomes the impenetrable sky. Turn your head to one side, and the lake becomes a wall right next to you, a churning, hazy, pleasant kind of wall, and you know that when it comes time to meet the Maker, you will have to pass through a wall that looks just like that. You will leave the air and the clouds and the dis-tant shore, and dive on through. And it won't hurt a bit.

Betty grew up along Highway 183, just north of Mendoza. Her daddy used to tell her she'd better watch herself before her ass grew to be the size of the Texas panhandle. He used to panhandle her some too, until one day she packed a bag and just walked clean away. The cowboy in the first dusty pickup told her she looked just like Betty Grable, hips, hair, eyes, and all--and so the name stuck.

Now Betty looks herself up and down before going out, checks the width of her rear against marks she made on the wall, just to see whether her daddy was right. She plucks the rollers from her hair and teases it out, and sure enough--Betty is right on time.

Betty has never needed any particular man. She does just fine on her own, thank you. Her daddy taught her at least that much. If you asked her what her needs were, she couldn't tell you. She likes to bring a man to that point when he just gets inside her, like a hound dog that can't wait to rush to its bowl, and she's happy to let him have it. That's when she feels the love wash right out of these men, like someone wringing out a great big mop. All their love washes into her, and she feels she's done right by herself. She likes to hear them say her name: *Oh God, Betty, oh Betty, my God!* She likes hearing her name alongside the Creator's. Then she knows her bed is a sacred place.

But it's not real, and she knows that too.

Betty's a good girl, really. And she's clean, she picks up after herself, takes care of herself. She brushes and flosses her teeth twice a day. While the man gets dressed to leave, she takes the time to wash. For him it's a little extra show just for free, and sometimes she makes it interesting. She struts herself a little as she's bending over the sink, lets the water drip a bit down her legs maybe, or, if she knows he's really watching, she'll wring the washcloth out at her throat, so that the water runs over her tits just as sweet as you please. Then she'll turn to him, coquettish, innocent, and ask some simple question like, "So you going straight home from here, honey? You be careful out in this heat, now. Yesterday I seen a tin can melt like a stick of butter."

Betty wishes she could do something constructive with her life, just a little something, like learning how to sew or crochet, or even taking care of a potted plant. Sometimes she envies the women she sees on the streets in the afternoon, the gals going into banks or the grocer's in their little white gloves and pressed suits.

The ones with children she tries not to see. But once she helped a woman whose baby had torn away from her and was *this close* to getting hit by a big old taxicab. Between the mother's wailing and the tires and the horn and the obscenities hurling all around, Betty managed to grab hold of the little tiger, dressed head to toe in baby blue and looking like a cornflower caught in an auger. The well-heeled little mother was by then squirting out crazy tears and wanting to hand Betty a twenty dollar bill. Betty didn't take the lady's money, but she patted the little one on the head and watched them walk away, a bit closer together than they had been before, and she wondered whether it was really true that she couldn't have children of her own.

Betty had learned one thing that day, though: her looks could stop traffic.

The men treated her as if they were her neighbors--and often they were. Betty felt comfortable around them. One of them liked to lay out his money on the dresser, patting it out with hands shaped by forty years of working the wells, and say things like, "Bitty grocery money for you there, darlin'," or "There you go, gal, you go get yourself that pretty blue thing they got in Jacobson's winder." Things he should have said to his wife before she went and died and it was all much too late.

Once she had gotten a job in the club next to her building, which was a little bit more steady. Sometimes she served drinks, or danced. The men would sway with her, with their big hands on her ass, and she would wiggle it for them. This is not to say that in public she was anything but a lady. Sometimes, when she saw someone who looked lonely or sad, she would just sit down and start talking to him. She'd say, "Shucks, I been dancing so much I could suck down the Gulf of Mexico if it weren't for the salt. Say, don't you look smart in that hat."

And that's all it took. He would turn to her gratefully, with a different kind of thirst in his eyes, and begin to drink her in. *Well now--* he might say, *How about could I get you something, Ma'am?* And she would reply with ease, and he'd smile and stick up his hand to make his order, and she'd cross her legs in just the right way, and then, before long, she might suggest they head on upstairs together.

It was nothing to her, a good deed of the day, to make a boy smile. Because that's what they became with her, boys again, once she paid them a little mind. A sixty-year-old widower, with full-grown kids that never called, could become a boy of eighteen, finding joy once more in something fresh, something comforting.

She could always see past their ages, past the physical distortions time had inflicted on them. She could always see who they really were, whether that was the man they used to be, or the man they still hoped to become, or the man they finally acceded to never becoming. These men would sit on the edge of her bed with their white legs and their pot bellies, and she would let them touch her under her satin shimmy, and let them put their fingers between her legs.

Oh, Betty would make you feel ten feet tall--or ten inches long, take your pick. Yeah, that Betty. She'd take you in and then take you in some more. Betty knew her stuff. She'd take you by the hand and set you down on that bed of hers, then she'd set herself on your lap and start opening up the buttons of your shirt real slow. And you'd have to crack some joke so she'd think you were just as comfortable as she was, even though your heart was in your throat and your hound dog prick was in your pants, seconds away from busting its leash.

And then she'd do this little strip, with you all comfortable on the pillow, and she and you would laugh together as she opened up her denim vest with the fringe hanging off it. Her bra would open in the front, and she'd wrestle that deal open in the blink of an eye--and that's exactly what you wouldn't want to do, blink. You don't want to miss a single slice of what she's serving.

Then you look at her, she's tickling you and arching her back, squeezing her arms, pushing those titties out where you can see them, and your hound dog is howling at the moon. And by the time she's got her sweet little pussy open for you--just you--all you want to do is give her every cent you got, and your coat and shoes too. "Oh my goodness!" she cries while she rides you. "Oh my! My, oh my!" Damn, Sam, take a moment and just picture that.

Yeah, who doesn't love Betty?

The men all had their stories: the first girl they ever made it with, that one touchdown, that one job offer, the day their first little one was born. They would tell her all their heart-aches too, about how life had mistreated them and left them high and dry. She began to amalgamate all the stories and images until finally she saw all men as one. Every man was the same. Same age, same hopes and dreams, same fears. And when they gushed inside her, with that pinched expression that made them seem like they were in harm's way, they even looked the same, every last one of them.

She had no choice but to fall in love with them all. Every man was her lover, her husband. And she was as faithful as any wife could be, and then some. When that door closed in the wee hours of the night and she listened to some man's boots going on down the stairs, the footsteps speeding up as they got farther away, she told herself he would be back tomorrow evening. He would always come back to her, and he would call her by her first name, like any husband would. *Betty,* he would say, *how are you, old gal? Been treating your-self right? How I love to see that smile on you, Betty. Betty, you know you're my girl.* The nights were cooler, and after he left, she could finally get her rest.

But then the day would come around, and with the unkind sun, the hard dawning that she was every bit as alone as they were.

Let me tell you, Betty was the finest thing around. But once in a while the heat would get to her, you know? And she would stay home, stay in bed with cucumbers on her eyes and lemons on her elbows. If you walked by her door, you might hear the quiet wail of an old record player:

Fly the ocean in a silver plane.
See the jungle when it's wet with rain
Just remember, til you're home again, you belong to me.

And you could imagine Betty in bed smoking maybe, not a thought showing on her face. If there were a tear in her eye, it was probably just from lying on her side too long. Betty never cries. Try knocking, though, and just see if that clunky old tap doesn't start running. *Sorry, didn't hear you sugar, must have been washing my hair when you stopped by.* The sound of water covers up a lot, if you think about it. It shuts out the world and keeps the world from finding out you don't always have the inclination to smile.

It was the daytime that hurt her the most--the heat, the light. When everybody else seemed to have some place to go.

The big-bright-big-bright bouncing in off the street like someone shouting out the hour. Made her thirsty, made her feel dry
and used up. Made her feel old.

But on good days the men would say *That's it, Betty,* as she
drew her pretty lips over their sturdy pricks. *Mmm,* as if she
hadn't had a man in years and years. *That's it girl. Good girl.
Oh, you come on up here now, come see Daddy, girl.* And she
would be happy again, and climb on up, and squeeze her nice
titties right up against their hairy chests where they liked it,
and imagine herself falling in love all over again.

Give it to me, Daddy. Do you love me, Daddy? Do you?

And then came Billy.

He was a sailor, so he was used to salt and swells and sea
breezes and stars that twinkled clearly overhead. When he
laid eyes on Betty for the first time, he knew right away not to
let her out of his sight again, that he and she had something
in common.

It was the night of the summer solstice, the longest day of
the year. Summer was just getting stoked, and already the grass
was burning. Betty was not having the best of days. She was
out of cash, hadn't eaten since the day before, and just managed to hop herself up on a stool and ask for a glass of water.

"Lady needs something a little stronger than that," came a
Gary Cooper voice from a dark corner.

Betty wheeled herself around and crossed her legs just so
out of habit, wicked patent leather boots sticking together
where they met. But her energy was sapped. "Water'll keep
me fine 'til it rains," she told the darkness.

"Shot of rye for the lady," said the voice.

She acquiesced. "Much obliged." She took her two glasses
and set them and herself down at the stranger's booth. The
stranger watched her drink the water first. She guzzled it so
fast she didn't even breathe.

They sat quietly for a few minutes, ignoring each other, gazing out at the empty bar. Betty fingered the little shot she still had before her. Then the stranger threw back his own glass, and so Betty did the same, without so much as a flinch. He seemed to smile at her. Betty seemed to smile back. And with a gentle cock of his head, the two of them were on their way.

He followed her home, yet lingered in her doorway, resting his hands on either side of the frame, letting his own interesting kind of heat seep into her room. Betty figured it was his cologne. She waited just inside the threshold, in front of his big open arms that seemed to bar her exit.

"You holding up the building?" she asked.

"You fixing to invite me in?" he asked.

For the first time, Betty was self-conscious. She smiled then, her pretty smile, the one that made most men melt into their boots, and gave him a little wink.

Billy was in her place, in her apartment. After all the others that had followed her inside, he was the first that made the place seem small. He's a big man, if you ever met him. But it's not like he takes up room, he just seems to fill a place. His steps were careful, but strong. Each move suited his purpose. When at last he had followed her around enough that she finally just quit moving away, they were standing beside her bed. Billy put his hands on her waist, and her stomach growled.

"Should I go get us something?" he asked, but she shook her head. "You got good hips on you, woman," he told her.

"Betty," she replied.

He bent his head down to her, so that his cheek touched hers. Betty felt overcome with him just being there, so close but not kissing her or anything. He just was. And bit by bit, she was too. They just were.

"Betty's not my real name," she said, for the first time ever.

He moved his head so that his scratchy cheek grazed down

around her chin and then came to rest upon her other cheek. His breath reached her ear, and Betty realized that he wore no cologne, but he still smelled good. "Hm," he murmured. "So what is?"

"I can't recall." And then she laughed, despite herself. Billy smiled.

"Well Betty, ain't you a tall drink of water on a hot day." And that was the moment he chose to kiss her.

The kiss frightened her. It made her think of scenes in movies, where even though you know it's coming, it still knocks the wind out of you and your eyes go soft and your body goes limp. It looks just great on a big screen, but when it's happening to you, in your own room, and you feel like all your bones have turned to syrup, and you still feel the imprints of leather-fine lips and the scrub of stubble against your cheeks and chin long after the kiss has reached its graceful conclusion--you have every reason to fear for your life. Because movies are just movies. This was real.

The only thing she had ever wanted was something real.

"You know this is going to cost you," she tried reminding him.

"Damn right, sugar."

He looked like he wanted to kiss her again, but instead he just kept his eyes on her while he put his two heavy fingers in the center of her chest. He opened up her little denim vest, then her bra, and let her stand like that in front of him. Billy sat down on her bed then, and just gazed up at her. Something about the light in that room--it was the lamp behind his head--it gave him a funny glow, like he was blessed or something. He just looked at her, and she wondered how she could be warm and cool at the same time.

He took hold of her hips again, and kissed her belly, a gentle, humble kind of kiss. Betty heard the patent leather of her boots crinkle. His hands went under her skirt, seeking her out. He asked her, "What's this right here, you got a soft spot for me, Betty? This a secret you're keeping? Lord, you are something, ain't you."

His two fingers were deep inside her, deep inside her barren womb, making it feel very much alive. "How's that? You like that, Betty?" he asked.

And she did.

They stayed like that for quite a while, making what might have sounded like polite conversation were it not for the occasional syllable that didn't quite fit in a dictionary. Billy's thumb also knew what to do.

But soon he lay back across her bed, dragging her with him, tugging at her clothes. Her feet got tangled up in her panties, and Billy kicked them away. He pulled her up and she thought he wanted her to wrestle open the big silver buckle on his belt, but he kept pulling on her and said, "Come on way up here, Betty, put your knees right here, lemme get a good look at you."

This was unusual; this was uncharted territory. He was teasing her, taking his own sweet time, taking control yet letting her know this was still her place, that she could kick him out any time she chose. Betty wasn't sure what to make of it, but then she was thinking about windmills and sawmills and oil wells and other things that are relentless and hypnotic and make you dizzy and make you want to lie down and weep. Billy's mouth could make a person melt dead away.

Those patent leather boots were making quite a scene on their own. Billy was holding onto them, passing his hands along them, keeping her where she needed to be. Finally, Betty felt like she was ready to drop right through that wall of water that led to the Other Side. But she fought it back and rolled off him, found a pillow and her breath.

"Jesus H. Christ!" she hissed.

Billy was in no sort of a hurry. He calmly rolled over next

to her and fell to stroking her body. Soft, easy strokes while he licked his lips. He kissed her again, and she felt as though she could never be whole again outside of that kiss. They wrapped their arms around each other like people in love, and their mouths made soft little noises.

Billy pulled his T-shirt over his head, and his jeans came off, and there was that profound moment of skin meeting skin. Betty felt good in his arms. Too good.

"Oh, you gotta get out of here," Betty told him, her voice choking over. "You gotta get going now. I don't like you."

"That so?" he asked, but he was kissing her throat, and she was raising her chin up so he could do it. Her skirt had bunched about her waist, and the heels of her boots were leaving cuts on the sheets. It bothered her a little. But Billy's hand was at her entrance, making sure the door was open.

And it was.

His body moved over hers and she lay weighted, suspended between him and the sagging mattress. The last thing Betty saw, as Billy's honest cock thrust home, was the image of a graceful tall ship, with four masts in full sail, leaning into the salt and spray--a tattoo where Billy's collarbones met one another. She felt the wind and water on her cheeks, and her eyes fell closed.

When she woke that first morning, with a slim shard of summer light invading the room, she was surprised to feel him get up and get dressed and to hear the door shut behind him. Not surprised that he had left, but surprised he had stayed as long as he had. Sad too. Sometime during that quick solstice night, as the earth's shadow made its closest path to the sun, she had actually begun to hope.

She had time to recall what had happened before they both fell asleep. She remembered the way Billy's cock had felt the first time he sank it deep inside her. It was as if he had said,

"Here, right here. This is where we both belong." Billy was a wall, a wall of hard flesh, and she clung to it, hung on for all she was worth. He had used his cock to get deep inside her, to communicate to her that she had nothing to fear, nothing to run from.

It didn't take but a minute before the two of them were connected by a thick glossy coating of perspiration. They glided together, the hardness of their bodies dissolving. Betty's limbs reached out, welcoming it all, every last drop of him--this man--and finally, she knew it was time to let go. She blinked back images of her daddy, images of the men she had known, all the aftershaves, all the colognes. She left the bright sky and the distant shore and dove on in.

And it didn't hurt a bit.

And afterward the two of them had kissed and washed at her sink. Billy hung his head upside down under the faucet and drank great mouthfuls of her rusty tap water, like a nomad who finally finds his desert oasis. And she did the same. And for once, she actually felt at peace. Refreshed. Slaked. Reborn.

They had taken turns washing each other until finally they were so cool and clean, there was nothing to do but get hot and dirty all over again. Billy hoisted her sweet bottom up into that sink, and the water spurted and bubbled and made funny sucking sounds and pooled on the tiles below. It sprayed up between them, soaking them both, beading on Billy's chest hairs, on Betty's lips and cheeks. They drank each other, drop by precious drop. And Billy's cock had told her again: *Here, right here. We belong just like this.*

But morning came all the same. The door closed behind him, and before long she was already starting in on washing her hair, getting ready to start again.

Start again.

The water was rushing past her ears. It dropped in warm

salty freshets from the creases of her eyes. It drizzled over the narrow bridge of her nose. Her tongue caught it in the little furrow above her pretty lips, lips that were stretched tight with the excruciating attempt not to cry. She coughed. Then again, violently. Betty's hands curled about her empty belly and her chin sank to her chest. Start again, gal. Get going now. Get shakin'.

No.

She felt a strong hand on her spine and froze, briefly fearful, but then not. She waited. Then there were arms around her, and a scruffy chin on her shoulder, and a towel falling to her ankles. Billy had come back ("Got us some doughnuts.") and was helping her with her hair. Helping her wash out the suds, the creme rinse. He brought fistfuls of water down over her back, and it dripped down her sides and dropped from her breasts. And he was naked and dripping behind her, and his warm wet hands were on her thighs, pulling them open, and he was deep inside her.

So good. Who would've guessed life could be so profound, so charmed? Not Betty. And now there she was, and there they were. Coupled, encased, absorbed into one another. She felt strong legs behind hers, and arms around her, and she felt Billy's strength mix with hers, and the thirst for whatever it was she had longed for all her life finally was appeased. She sobbed. She moaned. She wept hard. He was the gentle draft, the welcome sip. It's like when you're as thirsty as you can possibly be, and then someone hands you a frosty pitcher, and you can have absolutely all you want. You drink and drink, you guzzle it right down. You don't care who's looking, and you don't take time to breathe.

With his mouth full of doughnuts, Billy read to her from the morning paper, and she combed his hair for him, and they were kind of happy, like when there's a national holiday, and so you sleep in and take a day off for a change. Then Betty put her hair up in rollers and stepped out onto the fire escape.

Betty saw the city looming large through the grill beneath her feet, saw the ripples in the fabric of her life, distortions caused by the heat, and she felt real fear for the second time that morning. Made her think life was nothing but a mirage. But then Billy put his big hands around her waist and his rough cheek down close to her and said, "That stuff you put in your hair smells like bug spray," and she was compelled to twist in his arms and wrap her legs about him and let him carry her back inside, hips, hair, rollers, and all.

Billy didn't seem to ever want to go away, and that was a quality she liked in him. For a while some of her neighbors still complained about the water running a little longer than it should. But that was the sound of Billy treating her just right. It wasn't long anyway before the water stopped churning altogether, and the pipes in Betty's small apartment lay quiet for a good long time.

Strawberry Surprise
Clio Knight

The kitchen makes me feel sexy. I can't help it. Cooking inflames me, ingredients intoxicate me, the sound of sizzling steak turns my nipples into nuclear warheads. Making toast guarantees a hot flush at the very least, and the last time I put in a lamb roast I almost ravished the postman.

Maybe it's genetic. That would explain why Mum looks so satisfied when she puts dinner on the table.

Anyway, I woke up this morning thinking about strawberries. The best thing about being a freelance writer is you don't have to go into an office from nine to five. If you wake up feeling like strawberries, you can damn well go out and buy strawberries. So I did.

It's 10:00 a.m. and I'm back in my kitchen, carrying four baskets of the gorgeous things, all rosy red ripe and begging to be turned into something luscious. So many recipes, so little time...but I can't pass up strawberry shortcake. Crisp, soft sugary crust and whole, fresh berries glistening with syrup.

The morning sun floods our kitchen; between that and the

pre-heating oven, I'm starting to simmer. What the hell—I wriggle out of my shirt and toss it on the floor. I take off my bra, too. No sense in getting it all floury, and it's not as if anyone's going to disturb me—my flatmate does work nine to five. A few minutes later, my jeans join the growing puddle of clothes.

Shortcake crust is easy, it's just measuring and blending. It shouldn't take too much time out of my day—after all, I've got that travel article to write. The heat rising in the space between my legs undeniably intensifies as I stir flour into the creamy blend of butter, lemon juice, and sugar. The smell of the strawberries is driving me insane, and my breasts are crying out for physical attention. On impulse, I bite into a strawberry and brush the moist uneaten half over my erect nipples.

My flatmate walks through the front door. He looks surprised.

Mind you, I'd be surprised to find a topless woman in my kitchen. I'm a little startled myself. I finish off the strawberry, stalling for time. "Why aren't you at work?"

"I had a blinding headache. Funnily enough, it's not bothering me now." He gives me the weirdest look. "Are you cooking in the *nude*?"

"Not entirely nude," I say in a small voice. I'm hoping he has a sense of humor about this. He could kick me out if he wanted to—it's his place, I'm just the lodger. But if he was going to kick me out, he probably wouldn't be laughing so hard.

"You're so cute," he says when he finally stops laughing.

I'm surprised at this. I've been called crazy in my time, ridiculous, bizarre and occasionally sexy—never cute.

He crosses the living room slowly, so only the kitchen counter is between us. "Do you do this often?"

"That depends," I say cautiously, trying to keep my nipples out of his range of vision. "Is it forbidden in the lease?"

"Actually, I might make it compulsory." He grins that sexy grin of his that I noticed as soon as I moved in.

We don't see much of each other, since I'm out going after stories half the time, and he's stuck in an office, and in the four months I've been living here we've never flirted, not even once. I think it's some kind of record for me. And now I'm in his kitchen with my bare breasts on display and I can't help thinking how attractive he is. Maybe the strawberries *have* driven me insane.

Without taking my eyes off his, I pick up one of the strawberries and offer it to him. This way, we can be insane together.

He bites into the fruit, and his teeth are the sexiest thing I've ever seen. I suddenly wish I was fully clothed so he could undress me.

"So," he says, "what are you making?"

"Strawberry shortcake." He has a drop of strawberry juice on his lower lip. I stare at it, wondering if we're flirting yet.

"Really?" His voice is softer, more growly than I've heard it before. "I've always wanted to learn how to make that."

"If you come around this side of the counter, I could teach you." Yep, we're definitely flirting.

He moves slowly, stepping over my pile of discarded clothes. Now we're standing opposite each other in the tiny kitchen. It's a tense moment. He opens his mouth.

"Don't say it," I warn.

"Huh? Don't say what?"

"Don't ask to kiss the cook. It's a bad cliché, and it will put me off you for life."

"Oh." He grins that gorgeous grin of his, and my insides melt. "Actually, I was thinking about more than just kissing you."

Well, that's all right, then. No objections here.

His mouth is like honey, warm and sweet. His tongue laps inside my mouth, tasting me. I can feel him pressed against my panties, hard and getting harder. My hands curl into his zipper, tugging it open. "I should turn off the oven," I whisper.

"Fuck the oven," he mumbles, his mouth somewhere near my left nipple.

I decide to fuck him instead.

By the time we've dragged each other on top of the kitchen counter, I've managed to get his shirt off. These situations are so much easier if you start *without* clothes. His trousers end up somewhere about his knees, since neither of us can be bothered unlacing shoes at this point. I tease his jocks off slowly, then duck my head and take the length of him into my mouth. He groans, his eyes half closed and his head tipping back into a basket of strawberries. His hands reach down to caress my breasts, his fingertips trailing heat across my nipples.

After all that, it's my panties that give us the most trouble. Eventually he has to roll me on my back to remove them— and that's how I got strawberries in my hair. The bowl of shortcake mixture hits the floor, but I barely notice it falling. I'm too busy screaming and moaning because my back is jammed up against the saucepans, and his mouth is between my legs, licking and sucking me into another universe.

I could stay like this forever, but I'm greedy to have his gorgeous cock inside me. I wriggle out from under him and we roll across the counter together, kissing mouth to mouth. Suddenly he's thrusting down inside me and I thrust my hips up to welcome him in, screaming out as he fills me with shock waves of pleasure. I hope there aren't too many neighbors home at this time of day.

Keeping our balance on the counter is too much work. We end up on the floor, all sweat and strawberries, groaning in slow mutual rhythm. My legs are wrapped around him, pushing him further in. His breathing and his rhythm become more urgent, and as he finally releases into me with a deep groan, my insides explode with a burst of warm, sticky orgasm.

We're too exhausted to shower. We just tumble into my bed together, covered in crushed strawberries and each other.

It's hours before I can even think of moving. So much for that travel article.

Maybe I should be writing for the gourmet magazines instead— something about the seductive power of strawberries. It's probably a cliché. Maybe we should do something with raspberries next time.

I've got a fabulous recipe for summer pudding.

Cat and Mouse
Betty Blue

She was a pro. Cunt-red mouth parted over a set of teeth that could eat right through the television screen and into your lap.

"You've been a bad boy," said that mouth into the phone in the flickering video. How she could say that in a way that made you feel like your cock was being sucked, I don't know—well, I *don't* know, anyway, because I haven't got a cock, but at the first sound of her voice I pretty well imagined one sprouting up between my thighs and covered by her mouth. And from the expression on the face of the bad boy in question, I'm standing by that claim.

I'd seen a little porn in my day (not that my day was all that long, mind you, maybe six hours), but I hadn't ever seen anything like this. Porn stars were beach-ball breasted, waxed and shined, bleached, sprinkled with sparkles, and slick as candy; but this woman was *real*: punky black hair, seductively crooked mouth, a body like you'd want on your girlfriend, and slut-blacked eyes that could fuck you from across the room. The kind women at Good Vibrations had recommended her videos to me; thank you, ladies!

Her teeth—white, glistening seduction—were touching the black gloss of the phone, her bottom lip teasing against the rim, blood satin-red mouth curled into a sneer as she told that bad boy what she knew he wanted, and my hands were already discreetly between my thighs. The video had been on for thirty seconds.

"Wow." I just thought my roommate would like to hear my thoughtful review as we sat staring at the television together.

"*I know,*" she said.

I glanced up at her. I'd never heard her growl before.

The crank call was over now, and the porn star was swallowing a prick the likes of which can only be found in porn. She wasn't licking the head in an obligatory manner while yanking the spit-slick, lipsticked shaft in an approximation of a contracting throat. She was artfully, greedily swallowing her boyfriend's only-in-porn-dimensioned prick all the way to the 'nads. And smiling. This woman has muscles I never even knew existed. Then she was coming, and you could see it build as her legs shook appreciatively, and, *damn,* you could *hear* it build, like a real, live orgasm from a real, live girl, rocking the room as it sped up her toes and into her ass and straight up like an erection on the Invisible Man through her lips and her clit, and shooting up through her sweat- and come-soaked, non-beach-ball breasts until it burst out of those sticky, red, melted-candy lips and sharp, white teeth like a jackhammer in an empty warehouse pounding on steel.

"Wow," I said again.

"Unh."

There was no time for idle chat. The porn star was assfucking Bad Boy's wife. He had blindfolded his little suburban sweetie and told her to lie still, while unbeknownst to Sweetie, this thick-mascaraed power slut was climbing up on her from behind. We suspended disbelief as Sweetie bought that those soft, strong hands—tipped in violent red nails and snaking up her pert behind—belonged to hubby. (We were pretty much willing to give the slut goddess anything at this point, so what the hell was a little suspended disbelief?) I don't think we were breathing (okay, I lied; we were breathing so heavily that we could barely hear the T.V.) when the dangerous-looking fingertips parted those pert cheeks and—

"Oh, no; she's *not*—"

Oh, yes. She was. She'd produced a happy little gold wand, stuck it between those lucky lips and slid it straight up Sweetie's ass. There was no time to pretend not to be utterly thrilled by this. *Oh, well,* I thought, *there goes that secret kink.* (You have to understand that the roommie and I were raised Pentecostal. There were years of therapy and pretend-shock at the sight of ass-fucking still to work through.)

It was a painful eighty minutes, waiting politely, with damp panties, until we could dash back to our bedrooms and fully appreciate the film. I'd like to say we inched closer to one another on the couch, thighs warm, breasts heaving like marshmallow Peeps in a microwave, emitting soft moans, gasping but not jumping up like we'd been hit by a taser when our legs accidentally brushed together; that her hand slipped over my thigh in the red-blue glow of pornography and somehow her bra had fallen open and I don't remember where her shirt went, and I dove into her ample swells and sucked like there was no tomorrow; that she shoved me down on the dingy gold brocade couch somebody had left in my old apartment and that I insisted on dragging with me every time I moved ('cause "it's an antique, and it was *free!*"), and ripped the buttons off my shirt, if I happened to be wearing buttons, and yanked my bra out of the way and gave me what-for.

I'd like to say that we fucked like crazed hamsters, slipping and sliding and slamming fingers and tits and hips and clits, and ate the hell out of each other and came fifteen times, ejaculating twice, and went through every dick, dildo, and dong we had in our respective personal collections. I'd very much like to say all that (and I just have), but it wouldn't be true, no matter how great the material will be for my private gratification later this evening.

We were bi, we were friends, but we were simply not interested in ruining a perfectly good house-sharing arrangement and fifteen years of carefully cultivated friendship for an absolutely fabulous fuck. No, we saved that momentous falling-out for a few months later when every little spot on the rug and unwashed dish warranted a full-scale nuclear launch. Maybe we should have just gone for the sex.

So I didn't get laid that night—but I did have to change batteries at least once. The image of the pro, of that succulent, ripe plum of a mouth and those teeth that ought to be biting into one, stuck with me for years to come. It was a happy fixation that led me, indirectly, into the bed of my current lover. There's nothing like mutual porn-star infatu-lust for a solid relationship foundation.

When we were still casual acquaintances, he met and interviewed the porn star; I used it as an excuse to get him to come by my place so I could hear her voice on tape. As luck would have it, some months later the porn star came to town, and when she invited Jack to hang with her between sets at the strip joint, he let me tag along.

I don't have to tell you I was giddy. And nauseated. I'd never been to a strip joint, let alone "hung" with a porn star at one. It's not as if I hadn't seen strippers *at all*; I mean, for god's sake, I live in San Francisco. But having a sweet little cocoa-brown pregnant cutie wash my face with her tits at the *In Bed with Fairy Butch* cabaret with an appreciative crowd of cute dykes was a little different, a little safer, a little less...sticky.

We sat through a couple of sets before she came out;

enough time to relax (and get my face washed by a very nice cocoa-brown ass, with a bonus rub that made me want to ask how she got her pussy so smooth; hey, I'm a letch, but I'm practical). Then the waxy smell of theatrical fog announced our star, the headliner of the show.

She really was a pro. Where the other dancers had done halfhearted side-splits and grappled and slunk down the conveniently placed pole, yawning while they bestowed pussy-headlocks on the losers in the audience, she marched out on six-inch Lucite heels with sparklers and feathers and a tiny white sequined tuxedo. She worked the audience like a gracious slutty queen. I can't remember if she washed my face with anything; you'd think a girl would remember a thing like that, but I was a little giddy at the time—although I do have a picture of me holding her right breast.

But afterward, while visions of ripe plums danced in my head, and every word she uttered in her sultry voice sounded like, "Fuck me! Yeah! Yes, baby! Fuck that pussy!" and instead of her laugh I heard happy jackhammers on steel, I tagged along quietly to dinner, then dancing and drinks. It was the drinks that emboldened me. (Hell, it's always the drinks.)

So after the first half of my large glass of beer, I was feeling pret-ty cock-y, oh yeah. She commented on how nice my lover was to bring me along, and I said (and I'm feeling pretty clever about this, still, despite the fact that, *of course,* honey, if you're reading this, this *isn't true*), "Yes, he is. Of course, I'm just using him to get to you."

She laughed, jackhammers popped, and then—her tongue went down my throat. It's not nearly as cosmopolitan as it sounds, but, damn, for a few minutes, the ripe-plum lips and the ice-white teeth were baptizing my mouth, and I tasted the slut goddess's tongue. For a few seconds in time, I was the lucky brat at the end of her golden wand.

I was struck stupid, of course, but memories of the ride back to the club for her next set are distinctly impressed with the warmth of her cuddled against me in the back of the cab, her soft, strong hands snaking over my thighs—just playing with me absentmindedly as we shot through Tenderloin traffic, and chattering away in a voice that could raise the Titanic. It seemed like a friendly thing, just a couple of chicks cuddling in the warmth of a buzz in the back of a taxi on a Saturday night, but I couldn't help remembering a scene from one of her movies: the slut goddess riding in a limousine, drinking champagne in casual conversation while the big boss-man with a penis of gravity-defying proportions slips down between her open legs, unfettered by panties beneath her business suit skirt, and she rides his tongue through the dark city streets all night.

She had to rush to her next set; it was one in the morning, and my lover and I had some dancing of our own to do. I got one more soft, plum-lipped, warm-tongued kiss before she disappeared into the crowd of handlers backstage.

I may never get blindfolded and tossed facedown across a bed while a blood satin-lipped, dirty-talking, jet-black-haired punk of a slut goddess runs her tongue between my thighs and under my clit and snarls into my pussy while she eats it; or get slowly, smoothly fucked in the ass by a golden bullet-shaped dildo at her steady, red-tipped, and demanding hand until I'm moaning and screaming and writhing and bucking and willing to do anything for more; and I may never have my hair yanked back by the Joan Jett of porn and my face crammed into her cunt, and hissed at to "Eat that pussy, you bitch!" while I gratefully comply, my moans and sighs swallowed up by her slamming hips as she pitches toward the toe-curling, electric current of her jackhammering crescendo.

I may never kiss a porn star again...but I did, once.

Bad Girl
Alison Tyler

My ex-boyfriend and I used to play a game that seemed so naughty to me, I still blush at the thought. I'm sure other people have done worse, and I'm sure some folks will think it was nothing to feel guilty about. But to me, it was as if we'd crossed a line, some line of decency. After we played this game I would look at Paul with an expression of stunned satisfaction, pleased that we'd escaped a thunderbolt once again.

It's not that we were normally tame. From the beginning, Paul and I had a fairly wild sex life. He was a teacher at a high school in town, and we made love on his desk after the kids had left for the day. He spanked me. He tied me up. We fucked in public. I sucked him off while he drove. I fucked him at his mother's house. At a Christmas party, he took my cup of coffee into the bathroom, came into it, and brought it back to me. While I drank, he stood across the room, staring, excited to the point where he could no longer make idle conversation with those around him.

These activities paled in comparison to our brand-new game. It started while we were on vacation in the northern part of California. He'd rented a stone cabin in one of those old-fashioned vacation parks. There were twelve other cabins in the resort, all carefully spread out beneath a scattering of redwoods so that you felt as if you had the whole forest to yourself. Our little bungalow contained two beds, a small living area, and a kitchen. For some reason, and I still don't know why, I climbed into one bed and Paul climbed into the other. Maybe it's because it had been such a long day of driving. Maybe we were just playing around, as if we weren't going to fuck that night—unlikely for us. I rolled over, facing the wall, and stared at the pattern of the stones. Several minutes went by before Paul stood up and lifted the covers on my bed. As he climbed in next to me, he said, "Shhh, angel, we don't want Mommy to hear."

I froze. This wasn't our normal type of game. When we did S/M, he would talk dirty to me. He might say, "Lisa, you've been a bad girl, haven't you? Bad girls get spanked. Hold on to your ankles, and don't you stand up. Don't you flinch." He was the dominant, but he was always just Paul, my handsome boyfriend. If I played the role of a younger me, I was still me.

Now he said, "You be a good girl. You be nice for Daddy." I stayed totally still. His hands wandered between my legs, touching me through my panties, tracing the outer lips of my vagina. It felt good and bad and confusing, and I drenched my underwear.

"Uh oh," he said, "my little girl's all wet for me. Did you get yourself all wet for Daddy? Is that what you did?"

I couldn't answer. I just let him keep touching and stroking and playing. When he pressed up against my leg and I felt his hard cock, I thought that alone was going to make me come, that insistence of his cock brushing against my thigh.

"We have to be really quiet, Lisa," he said softly. "Mommy's asleep in the other bed, and we don't want to wake her. Then she'd know what I know. She'd know just what a bad girl you are. What a sinful little girl you are. I'd have to punish you severely if she ever found that out. Do you understand me?"

I nodded.

"Good girl," he said, "That's my good girl."

He spooned against me, lifting my nightgown, lowering my panties, and entering me from behind. His hands wandered over the front of my nightgown, cupping my breasts. He pressed his lips to my ear, whispering, "My girl is getting so big now, isn't she? Look at the way your breasts fill my hands." He rubbed my nipples against the flat of his palms and they stood at attention, poking against the flannel fabric of my nightgown. "Yes, she is. Nice and big for me. And look at how hard your little nips get. I only have to brush them lightly."

His voice was a husky whisper, as if he were honestly trying to keep quiet. His cock throbbed inside me, and he brought one hand to the front of my body, raising my nightgown and placing his fingers against my pussy. He pressed against me, finding the wetness, then locating my clit and sliding his fingers over and around it. I moaned at the sensation, and instantly he hissed, "Didn't I say to be quiet? We're going to have to go outside behind the house for a little punishment session if you can't control yourself. Look over on that chair, Lisa." I turned my head slightly. "See Daddy's belt?" I murmured an assent. "I'm going to have to tan your bottom with that belt if you can't keep yourself under control. You know what that feels like, don't you, girl? Don't you know what it feels like to have your bottom thrashed by my belt?"

His fingers played me. They stroked up and down, and I tried so hard to do what he said, to be quiet and behave. I'd never been that turned on before. Not when he used masking tape to bind me over one of the little desks in his classroom, slapping the wooden ruler on my naked haunches. Not when we snuck off at his sister's wedding and fucked during the reception. This was it. My pinnacle. The dirtiest thing I could think of, and it made me weak. I didn't moan again, but my breathing came hard and fast.

"You need to be quiet," he said in that hushed, menacing tone. "Daddy gets so tired of having to punish you. Why can't you be a good girl, Lisa? Why can't you be good for me, like your sister?"

That did it. That made me come. Sick and twisted and over the top, I leaned back against him and let the riptide of orgasm slam through me. He gripped his arms around me, bucking faster and faster until he reached it, too, pulling out to come all over my backside, holding me tight so I couldn't turn around to face him, to see whatever expression of horror would reflect my own. What had we done? What had we just done? What line did we cross? Where would we go from here?

"Bad girl," was all he said, lips against my ear. "I always knew you were a really bad girl, Lisa. And bad girls get punished. Why don't you go over there and get my belt so we can deal with this? Go on and get it for me. You know you deserve it, Lisa." He shook his head. "Such a bad little girl."

Bad girl, I thought as I stood and walked to the chair. That's what I am. That's what I was the whole time, I just hadn't known it for sure.

London Derrière

Dawn O'Hara

Never perform with your back to the audience, Orlando taught his rare music students (he took on such a commitment only when financially desperate). Shaking your booty works if you've got Jon Bon Jovi's ass, he instructed, worthy of leather encasement and admirable even from the back row of an arena. But if you are a mere mortal crooning in a local pub, best to face the fans.

How, then, did Orlando come to find himself bent over a barstool on the stage floor—nothing more than a bar corner cleared of tables—with Isabella's dick up his forty-one-year-old virgin ass? His back to the audience, indeed.

Orlando now sang a different tune than the melodic ones he'd played for the small audience of late-nighters. His voice lost its smooth patina. His words contained no witty double entendres, looping rhymes, or seductive repetitions. He abandoned his lyrical search for meaning in a complicated world of misunderstood words. His fingers no longer picked at intricate chord progressions on the six-string or the electric keyboard. They clawed at the air. He growled and shouted, his words incomprehensible, pushing back against Isabella's thrusting thighs. But before he descended into passionate, guttural urges, his words were clear.

Orlando feared the peculiar combination of words he shouted. He was terrified that, once they were uttered, Isabella would have what she wanted and would leave him. Again. Only this time she would desert him for speaking the irretrievable, not for silence.

Hold something back, Orlando taught. Leave them wanting, so the fans return--or, better yet, purchase the CD you've peddled for years, stacks of them stashed in your attic. The whole song can't be a repeating chorus, he insisted. You've got to build up to the consummate word at the end of the line. A literary crescendo to a word so perfect that the audience thinks they could have guessed it, but a word so unexpected they never do. They echo it once they've heard the song, and then forget the wonder and surprise of it. Like this word he just enunciated as clearly as "The Rain in Spain before deteriorating into whimpering gibberish. A word that all too often atrophied, stalled, and lost its meaning through overuse. A powerful word that dulled and tired. Coveting words, understanding their potency and deception, he had refused to utter it all these years.

Now that he'd said it, held nothing back, Isabella would leave him with his cock dancing in the air. Something prevented him from seizing his straining dick, which beseeched the stale barroom air like a blind man extending his cane over a bluff. One clench of his fist and Orlando would add to the stains on the floor, he was that close to the edge of primal fulfillment. Isabella hadn't told him not to touch himself, though she often commanded him in bed. Orlando himself was never comfortable articulating what he wanted done to his body, and he graciously accepted what was offered. But right now he wanted his satisfaction—if she planned to give him any—to come at her hands, the gift of her body. He'd had enough of his own fist since she'd kicked him out a month ago.

As Isabella brought up the rhythm section behind him, the logistical success of this joint venture amazed Orlando. But, then again, they'd always enjoyed the challenge of different body sizes. He tended to forget how small she was. Her ass gave her such solidity, a gravity-hugging mass—like a steel girder that holds up a delicate bridge, one of those impossible pieces of architecture that tourists traverse the world to see— that he often forgot that his long fingers could nearly span her petite waist. Sometimes when he spied her tiny shoes kicked off at the front door, he wondered who'd come to visit.

Isabella's ass. Now *there* was a show fit for stadium concerts. Forget the rules about facing the audience. Her magnificent flesh danced in multiple directions when she moved. Some law of physics or aerodynamics caused one hemisphere of her buttocks to return from movement while an opposing quarter gained momentum in the opposite direction, the way two stones tossed into a pond throw concentric circles into delirium. Her gluteals were like tectonic plates beneath the earth's surface, the mountains above them trembling and quaking when they shifted.

When Orlando was still a young man, years before Isabella backed her ancient Cadillac into his Toyota, one of his dates had blubbered over the televised royal wedding of the worthless second-in-line son to the worthless British throne. Somewhere in her tears, Orlando saw the crushed belief that even though the firstborn prince had escaped her, the second son had still roamed in her fantasies as a distinct possibility. She, an American. From Detroit. He had waited impatiently for the "I do"s so they could head to dinner. And then he'd caught sight of the bride's well-padded ass behind an oversized satin bow. He could have watched the princess march up the aisle for miles. He wanted to reach up inside her gown and caress those buttocks, to crawl after that fanny through the church and into eternity with his hands groping. Her ass wasn't even *that* big, except in comparison to Barbie dolls like her new sister-in-law. When radio deejays made cruel Mount Everest and Twin Peaks remarks about her behind, Orlando knew that not one of those men voicing loud derision over the princess's flanks would turn down the chance to feel her ass bouncing against his belly, his cock lost in the valleys only mountains like hers could provide. A guy's dick could seem awfully small and insignificant rutting around a generous ass, and Orlando suspected their taunting was born of that insecurity. Orlando thanked whatever cosmic force had blessed him with the long and narrow cock ideal for such excavating, a highly evolved instrument honed for intricate maneuvers.

Orlando and his date never did get to dinner that night. They ordered in, and he had barbecued rump roast right in her bed. It wasn't the start of a fetish, exactly, or even an obsession. Orlando liked women of all sizes—but big-hipped women became synonymous with royalty in his plebian mind. That bow on a princess's palatial behind tied a permanent knot around his preference, and he remained married to the idea of someday finding his own monarchial mounds to worship.

But Orlando soon learned that these splendid endomorphs didn't crave worship of the twin-buttressed cathedrals on their backsides. Rather, they wished to crush these sacred temples, as ancient peoples had smashed shrines glorifying opposing religions. They wanted to destroy these icons of femininity, praying for the holiness of honed and toned hind-ends. They wanted him not to pay homage to the bouncing, mirrored embodiments of his faith, but to ignore them, converting to a belief in slender flanks held in by Control Top hosiery.

When the princess crash dieted later on and became the spokesperson for a diet product, Orlando composed a dirge. Her lost flesh symbolized the war waged upon the tortured landscape of women's asses, a genocidal campaign for the extermination of something holy. His lovers all felt rotten about not being Twiggy. He craved the sight of their haunches wriggling, but these ripe, succulent women extinguished the lights and crawled under the covers, face up in the dark. Which is why, with the passage of years, he seldom followed through on his attraction for them. He swore them off, a gluteal abstinence, the way friends with wheat allergies had given up gluten. Their constant need for reassurance wore him down. They vacuumed up his repeated compliments, and then ceased to believe them precisely because of their repetition. Ah, the trickiness of words.

Then Isabella had climbed out of her mammoth automobile a few years ago after reversing into his hatchback. When she leaned across the seat to dig her insurance card out of the glove box, her derrière sticking out of the car door, Orlando swooned. Such an ass could sing opera. No little Mimi or Butterfly pining for her straying dude, either, but a ferocious and tender Turandot demanding the severed heads of unworthy suitors. Orlando stuttered so ferociously when she approached that Isabella thought he'd had a concussion from the minor accident. He'd bruised his forehead on the steering wheel with her lurch into reverse, yes—but all he wanted was to smash his face against those cheeks, just the way his hood had crumpled under the staggering weight of the Cadillac's trunk. He wanted bumper imprints ground into his deliriously smiling front grille. He reminded himself that he had given up on these women, sworn them off in a permanent Lent. The simplicity of a glorious derrière had too often trapped him in complicated and ugly arguments. When he wanted a fistful of those mounds, he usually got an earful about his inability to understand. He didn't blame these women for their insecurity; they were the victims of a modern witch-hunt for body fat. But despite his devotion to their ample order, Orlando could not resurrect a religion based on his cock alone, and so went on a flesh fast.

He could have abstained, he lied to himself, if Isabella hadn't spoken in that damned accent, refined aristocratic education crossed with Monty Python crass in her Oxford gutter mouth. A dethroned British queen had backed into him, and he wanted her to keep backing up, rolling her glorious bulldozer of a behind right onto the cock pulsing in his lap. He bulged so prominently that he refused to get out of his squashed bug of a car. She feared that he couldn't extricate himself from the interlocking, twisted metal of the two cars--and it was true in a way; his heart remained trapped by her rear end. His lustful frame of mind was permanently bent to her shape.

The dreadful sound of the two vehicles wrenching apart, Isabella with her foot on the gas, this time in first gear, was not as painful as the silence after she drove him out the front door last month, suitcase and guitar in hand.

She drove him home that first afternoon, but said she was so rattled she needed to stop for a drink. She declared he looked like he needed one, too. She drank her double whiskey in regular cola. "None of that diet crap," she warned the bartender.

After three beers, Orlando couldn't help it: he began to hum "Londonderry Air." He made the words up on the spot, and the revised "London Derrière" began spilling out. She might have socked him in the jaw, but instead she laughed, delighted. She dragged him onto the dance floor and gyrated, her back against him. This time he could not hide his eager gearshift behind a bent steering wheel. They hooked together like a tow-hitch and its load. He wrote her a new song on each anniversary of their crash. "Do the Locomotive." "Fanny Fandango." "Mother Goose Your Caboose." "Let's Cause a Rumpus." The songs were for her only, hymns performed during private services to her body. But on their fifth anniversary, she didn't want a song. She wanted a three-word sentence.

He admired the way she dressed—or didn't. Not attired in a flowery potato-sack to hide her figure or a blouse tight on the boobs to distract from the rest of her. No obvious and generally futile attempt to disguise the fact that she wore a jeans size in double digits, twice her blouse size. "Vertical stripes aren't going to fucking fool anybody," she said--not that she cared to. She wore bright, bold colors and patterns, and snug fits. Not tight or restrictive, but contoured to her shape. Mostly, though, Isabella went naked, stripping with relief as soon as the front door closed behind her.

Isabella didn't need convincing or wooing to bend over for him. After cocktails, she took him to her house without asking where he wanted to go. Bedroom curtains open, Isabella offered herself like one of those monkeys on The Discovery Channel. He approached the twin celestial planets that orbited around her fiery core with reverential hands. Just as he had once caressed Jimi Hendrix's left-handed guitar, the curves so like Isabella's; as he had stroked the Buddha's belly in China; as he had held his first erection in wonder and terror. He spread her cheeks apart. He broke Lent. He lost his cock in her cosmic folds, a tiny spaceship careening through her vortex. The puckered crater of her asshole winked up at him from between her double moons.

With the lights blazing, he got to watch his fingers digging into her hips, circles of white spreading from his grip. It was like denting a tender peach, or watching the impression of his foot on wet sand. He seized her jiggling ass to hang on, like a roller coaster handle, wanting to bruise it with the force of his grip. He reached around to lolling breasts and thighs spread just right for easy access to the magic spot so many men, apparently, ignored. Why? It was so easy. He'd seen the way women worked over his dick, with mouth, hand, or body. Jesus, making him come took *effort*. But he could just lie back, one arm under his head, and move a single finger.

Even a pinkie. Even a goddamn toe positioned just right, though it tended to cramp up on him if she took awhile—and Isabella was never one to hurry. Yeah, sometimes it was an afterthought—face it, he could be as quick and eager as the next guy, he was no god—but the gesture was one they sure appreciated.

Orlando carefully kept one of his fingers uncalloused. His love digit, Isabella christened it. All it takes is one, his first girlfriend had taught him, a piece of knowledge that had served him better than anything he'd learned in college. Keep it clean and well trimmed, she'd said, and that way you can put it just about anywhere. Later, after he'd picked up the steel-string and welts of protective skin cropped up all over his hands, he left one fingertip smooth. Only good for picking his nose, he told his vapid-eyed music students. It hampered complicated riffs, but the sacrifice was worth it.

Like the perfect lyric, Isabella continually surprised him. Shunning the girdle-ish contraptions other women trapped themselves in, Isabella wore thong underwear—when she wore any at all. She claimed panties wouldn't fit her, other than the suffocating type she had no interest in wearing. Instead of plucking at elastic that climbed uncomfortably, she let it all hang out. Her undies were no more than a swatch of fabric that cupped her *mons*, and a string that nestled where Orlando wished his tongue could take up permanent residence.

Isabella let him watch her shower, the soap disappearing between the cleavage of her thighs. She bathed belly-down in the oversized tub she'd remodeled the house around, her ass mounds looking like twin atolls rising out of the bubbly deep. Amelia Earhart's plane could vanish in that landscape. Isabella declared she would never need a tattoo, since Orlando's ass hickies permanently decorated her. He couldn't help nibbling his devotion, a taking of the sacrament. As soon as one love bite faded, he replaced it with another. She backed up to mirrors, contorting impossibly as she tried to find Rorschach meaning in their patterns.

On the rare occasions when Orlando refused to be distracted from practicing by her undulating waves of desire, Isabella practiced naked yoga in his line of vision. Her wide-hulled boat continually capsized during the balancing poses. His willpower couldn't surmount such a tidal effect, and before she'd toppled over a third time, he gave in to temptation and righted her with his sturdy mast.

He'd been surprised when she'd packed his things a month ago. (There was no question as to who would stay, as he could never ask her to give up the bathtub.) She abdicated the throne he'd constructed beneath her. Left him a country-less peasant, an expatriate wandering through the pages of disappointing swimsuit issues. All because of one word. One stupid word. What a tragic irony, fit for an opera, that his song lyrics had wooed Isabella to him, but his silence in response to her demand had driven her away.

Dumping him looked good on her. He couldn't take his eyes off her once he'd spotted her precariously perched on a barstool. He wanted to metamorphose into that stool. She looked like she'd swallowed the goddess she always sprinkled into casual conversation. She looked powerful. She looked like trouble. Dressed to kill in a red Empire-waist dress that cinched her bodice but flared out at the hips and fell past her knees, she looked like the Great Pyramid. Not one of the Egyptian queens mummified inside, no, but a live monument pulsing with desert sunlight, stretching to the sky yet rooted on earth, radiating heat.

Isabella always looked damned hot walking away. Trailing behind her at the mall or the market, admiring her bouncing globes, Orlando often felt he would have been a better student with such visual aids.

But Isabella looked even better coming towards him.

"Isabella." He spread his hands when she approached him after the last song. She needn't have waited so politely—she was an audience of one.

"You're an asshole," she said in her irresistible accent.

"I know." He would do or say anything tonight to get her back.

"No, you don't. I'm going to make you *feel* the meaning of asshole. So that next time you'll think twice before using it on someone else."

"Hey, I did *not* shit on you."

"No, because you're emotionally constipated." She seemed surprised by her own wit.

He spied the crack in her slammed door, the thin moment where he could sneak in and make her forget her anger. "Can I use that in a song?"

"Always a joke. Always your music." She hung on to her resentment, leveraging herself against the other side of the door, her side of the argument. "Always detachment. Reserve. Calculation. Tonight I'm breaking your barrier. Drop your pants, asshole." But she lifted her skirt, exposing herself to the waist.

"Jesus." His mouth dropped open, not his 501s. Instead of damp and miniscule panties, curlicues of wiry hair escaping along the creases of her hip, he saw that Isabella had sprouted a penis. It seemed as if their entire courtship had been a buildup to the lyrical surprise of the pink and white swirled cock *springing* from beneath her uplifted dress. Strapped on with a complicated series of belts and buckles, the cock appeared lifelike in shape, if not in color. The straps looked damned uncomfortable, cutting into her generous flesh. He admired her ease with the contraption. Most women of her build wouldn't be caught dead in a bikini, much less this getup. Her thong was proving entirely inadequate to the task of restraining the hungry beast.

"Isabella, what the hell do you want?"

"I want your hymen."

Hi, men! His mind spun spellings and alternate definitions. His mental wordplay always got worse when he was nervous, a subconscious tic he couldn't control. "Whoa, whoa, whoa."

"I want your cherry. Your maidenhead."

He stepped backwards, away from the threatening member. "This is a joke, right?"

"You're looking at the punch line." She took the hefty pink cock in her small fist. "Take a good look while you can, because you're not going to be seeing much of it the rest of the night."

Ironically, Isabella had never seemed less womanly than with this jutting member thrusting forward from her thighs, her queenly power visibly concentrated in this vengeful scepter. Orlando was hot. Inflamed. Also terrified.

"Isabella. Christ. Here?" He glanced around the deserted bar. The bartender had started to set the chairs on the tables halfway through Orlando's last set. His mediocre and distracted performance once he'd caught sight of Isabella in the audience had encouraged few to remain through to the last number. The bartender had waved goodnight before Orlando's last note faded, calling out for him to lock up on his way out, adding that he'd mop in the morning, unless Orlando wanted to do it for extra cash.

"All the better if someone sees you for the asshole that you are," Isabella said.

"Fine! Fine." Orlando tore at his belt buckle and thrashed his pants to his ankles. "I'll play your little game. Whatever you want, Isabella." He turned his back to her before lowering his boxers, so she couldn't see the eager state of his cock. Orlando didn't know if he was angrier at Isabella or at the betrayal of his own dick, which rose up in direct opposition to what he thought he didn't want. But he did know that he wanted her to stay, to connect with her. On any level. He bent over the barstool he'd perched on for his show and reached around to spread his asscheeks. "Come and get it."

Her dress rustled as she stepped close behind him. He smelled her, an oasis of bubble bath-clean in a stale swamp of cigarette smoke and beer.

"You know what I want," she said, the tip of her dick hovering in his delicate pucker.

"Why is it so important?" he shouted over his shoulder. "Christ, you *know* how I feel. Isn't it more important that I *show* it? *Express* it? Don't I do that?"

She pressed deeper, the tip of her cock just kissing the tight fist of his asshole. "I want you to say it."

He grunted. "It can't possibly mean the same thing to different people."

"You're holding back out of fear. Just like with your music. You won't commit the last three percent. That's why you're still playing dives like this."

"We've been over this a thousand times. It's worthless to say it."

The tight bud of his asshole opened at her nudging insistence. "I know it's what you feel. Just say it."

"It's meaningless if you have to ask."

"It's everything."

He made an incoherent noise as she slipped in a centimeter, then another. Isabella still worked with metrics.

"It won't kill you," she said. "Don't be afraid."

"I'm done talking. You... uhn, you just do what you have to do to make your point."

"I'm not stopping 'till you say it."

Crafty Isabella had just thwarted herself. Her cock crept its slow, methodical way into his body; Orlando didn't want her to stop. Considering his preoccupation with rear ends, it now struck him as odd that he'd never considered his own. His morning post-coffee toiletries and a vigorous scrubbing were all the attentions he'd ever thought of bestowing upon it.

"You're pressuring me," he quipped, disguising his level of enjoyment with the sort of response that had incited her to this in the first place.

She slapped his ass. "Say it."

Orlando was silent.

Slowly Isabella worked her slippery dick in. She was being careful, he could tell, cautious not to really hurt him. His ass now pressed firmly beneath the swell of her belly. The front of her thighs nudged the back of his. Her high-heeled feet, calculated for the height she would need for this maneuver, were wedged between his scuffed cowboy boots, swathed with his jeans and boxers like the base of a Christmas tree. Orlando had never experienced the blindness of having someone make love to him from behind, never felt the surprise of every touch by their hands or body. Isabella often mounted him while he lay on his back, telling him to hold still until she'd used him for her own friction, but he could still participate, teasing between her legs or massaging her breasts, communicating with facial expressions. This was powerlessness of another order. Total abandon, at her mercy. An absolute trust and giving of oneself. And she had done it so boldly, so baldly, so often.

She grabbed fistfuls of his scant hips, and leaned over to whisper in his ear. "Say it."

Orlando pushed back against her.

Isabella began to fuck him in earnest. Her breath changed to short pants of hot steam on his back. Her movements became more calculated. She had gone from anger to arousal. He sensed her surprise, that this fucking would afford her pleasure, too. She picked up her pace, forgot the metric system and took a quantum leap. Isabella gave him her last three percent, going deep.

She grabbed his hair. "Say it!" She punctuated her repeated demand with the insistent sound of her belly slapping against his ass. If someone had peeked through the steamy front windows into the dim bar, all they would have seen was the flapping red tent of her dress, the spread wings of an exotic bird.

Orlando opened his mouth but couldn't catch his breath.

"I love you," Isabella said softly. She broke through his barrier with her thrusts.

"I...Damn it, I love you," Orlando half sobbed. She had burst some dam within him. Some massive, concrete structure that had allowed only trickles of truth to get through, leaving those on the other side thirsty and parched. The granite crumbled, and years of pent-up, churning water deluged the desert. "I do. I really do."

Isabella abruptly stilled.

"Don't stop! Don't."

"Say it. Say it."

"Jesus," he bit his lip. "I fucking love you. I fucking love you. Oh, god, fuck me, I love you. Christ. Let me love you."

She was right about his music, about everything. He had cassette tapes crammed with serious songs. Lyrics that expressed his ache and longing and, yes, his love. But he feared they were sappy, that he would be laughed at, and so he made laughter at his humorous songs a certainty. No risk. Isabella's thrusts knocked those tunes loose, setting free a flock of singing birds in his head. Stored up inside him for years now, they tumbled out.

"I love you, I love you, I love," he said, in time with her thrusts. He knew her sounds, could tell how close she was. She slapped against him, harder and faster. He was so full of her, to the depths of his core, that he could hardly stand it. And he couldn't believe it, but he was coming. Without a touch from her on his cock, he was coming, too. He cried, and came, shouting that he loved her. She burst, and he burst, and they stood shuddering. The red dress shimmered with the trembling of their joined bodies.

She played with his hair and nibbled on his shoulder, her arms tight around his belly, her breasts smashed against his back. He didn't want this moment to end. He didn't want her to ever pull herself out of him. He wanted her to take up residence in his guts.

Except that then he would never have another good look at her ass.

Red Lace Teddy
Celia O'Toole

I pull the red lace teddy out of its hiding place in the back of the drawer and finger the satin-covered buttons. I'm feeling horny and sexy, and whenever I feel that way, I'm drawn to wearing racy lingerie.

That outfit just doesn't do much for me. I hear your voice in my head, admonishing me as I hold the teddy up to my torso. I run my hand down the lacy bodice. *It's too scratchy,* I imagine you complaining—but what you call scratchy feels sensuous and exciting to me. The texture has a *there-ness* to it, a responsiveness that says, *Hey, notice me. Experience me.* My fingertips accept the invitation; they tingle, traveling in stops and starts over the thready edges of the lace.

Already I feel a warm wetness in my crotch as I imagine the lace against my skin. Electricity jolts my nipples as I think of fingers tracing the lace above them.

I know this isn't your thing, I imagine myself arguing with you, *but I want to wear it for* me. I strip naked and slide the teddy up past my hips and bring the satin straps over my shoulders.

I stare at myself in the mirror. I'm my own best audience, I suddenly realize. I guess you won't tell me, so I tell myself that I look hot, exceptionally hot. Hot, delicious, and downright delectable. I admire the scandalously red fabric that simultaneously reveals and conceals. I like the way the lace lightly hugs my curves; my physique virtually screams sexuality. The high-cut leg openings are an invitation to touch. My barely covered breasts are begging to be revealed and sucked. I turn around and admire the low-cut back and thong-like strap that fastens at the crotch. My buttocks cry out to be stroked, and I imagine your hands, cool and dry, doing so as you kiss me and press me hard against your bulging pants.

Yes, I know that you don't get turned on by lingerie. But in my fantasy, I need a seductee. You get to fill that role. So I fantasize some more about your hands--grabbing my buttocks, almost lifting me in your urgency to position my cunt closer to your cock. In my fantasy, your passion takes my breath away.

I turn to face the mirror again. I'm so hot that this vision in the red lace getup makes me want to fuck *myself*. I decide that I will—but slowly.

Wearing the teddy underneath, I put my clothes back on. I decide that I won't tell you what I'm wearing—no need to make you feel uncomfortable or afraid of my expectations. This is for *me*.

I imagine the evening that we'll spend together, you thinking that we're having our usual Saturday night movie date, me spending the entire time becoming more and more aroused.

Every time I move, I'll feel the lace slide against my skin. The scratchiness that you object to will provide just the right amount of stimulation to remind me what I'm wearing. When I reach to set the popcorn on the movie theater floor, I'll feel the stretch of the lace against my side to remind me that my nipples are covered in lace. And then they'll harden and I'll sit straighter in my seat to tighten the pressure of the teddy against them. I'll twist slightly from side to side. You won't even notice, but I'll actually be using the lace to play with my nipples, making them harder with each tiny movement.

When I settle down into the theater seat, I'll feel the teddy's narrow crotch strap work its way into my ass crack and pull against my cunt. I'll feel a patch of wetness gather there and I'll have to restrain myself from making humping movements right there in my seat.

It's too bad that you don't get turned on by lingerie, because this is fun.

Every time you put your arm around me, you'll be pressing against the lace, and you won't even know it. Without "regular" underwear on, I'll feel naked, and each touch from you will be like a tease. If you put your arm around my shoulder, I'll silently will your hands to move a few inches and tweak my nipple—even though I know you won't. When we're walking together and you put your arm around my waist, I'll silently will your hand to move lower and stroke my nearly naked ass—even though, again, I know you won't. With each reminder of my state of undress, I'll become more excited. My cunt will become more and more swollen, until, by the time we head home from the movies, it's throbbing.

The trick will be how to orchestrate what happens once we get home. I won't be done with the teddy yet. It will have been part of my foreplay and I won't be done fucking myself yet. So I'll invite you to come to bed early. I'll kiss you *that way*—the way that tells you I'm already aroused, so that what's coming will be lots of fun and very little work for you. I won't let you follow the usual efficient bedtime routine of putting on pajamas, brushing your teeth, turning out the lights, climbing into bed, and fucking last, if at all. I'll say that I have something to tell you.

I'll be nervous, shy, apprehensive. I'll be about to confess that I've been masturbating right under your nose for the last several hours. Maybe you'll find it a turn-on, but maybe you'll think I'm perverted. So I'll be scared--but I won't let it stop me.

I'll drag you onto the bed and we'll neck until you get hard. Then I'll tell you what I've done. As I talk, I'll grind my crotch into yours. I may even push you down on the bed, straddle you, and dry-hump you. I know you don't like the scratchy lace, so I won't take my clothes off while I still have the urge to touch you. But by the time I'm finished touching you, I'll be so wet that it will have seeped through to my jeans.

Then I'll ask, "Do you want to watch me fuck myself?" Of course, most of the foreplay will have already happened—so what I'll mean is, do you want to watch the final stretch?

You'll probably say yes, so I'll take off my clothes. I'll invite you to take yours off, too, and you'll probably ask me how I want you. I'll say that I want you naked because I want to see your cock and I want to watch you touch yourself. So you'll get undressed.

When I'm stripped down to my teddy, I'll run my hands up and down the lace, just like I did earlier. Only this time, I'll be so much more turned on. I'll pause at my nipples and pinch them through the lace, then pull the teddy off my shoulders to expose my breasts and pinch and pull at my bare nipples.

As I continue to work my nipples with one hand, I'll slide the other one over to my sopping, waiting cunt. My lips will be so swollen, the thin strip of lace won't be able to contain a thing. I'll slide my fingers into my slippery slit and stroke myself until I moan.

You'll complain that you can't see what I'm doing, so I'll pile up some pillows, lean back on them, bend my knees, and spread my legs wide. Still wearing the teddy, I'll play with my cunt until I'm howling, rubbing my clit through the outside of the lace, slipping my fingers underneath, alternately stroking and finger-fucking myself as the puddle of juices underneath me grows. Then, since you'll still be frustrated because you can't see everything, I'll strip the teddy off and continue to fuck myself, free of encumbrances.

I'll watch your cock grow harder and bigger and I'll want it. Now that I'm naked, you won't be able to resist plunging yourself into me. I'll move over and straddle you, like we did clothed, only this time without any fabric barriers to impede us.

I'll impale myself on you--hard, fast, and wet--and that first thrust will make me holler with delight. I'll fuck you furiously, screaming when I come. Then I'll pull you over on top of me, because I'll want to feel you driving yourself into me. You'll do just that, pounding with enthusiastic pleasure until you start to come. My insides will open up to you and you'll fill me as we come together in one final, shattering orgasm.

It's too bad that lingerie doesn't do much for you. It sure does a lot for me.

The Trouble with Claws
Jean Roberta

I am too soft and submissive–sometimes, anyway. Or else I am not a true lesbian-feminist.

Pressing fake fingernails onto my real ones, I wonder if other women actually enjoy wearing these things. Centerfold models flash their hard red nails at their soft pink or tan or chocolate curves: *look at this*. The viewer is supposed to see those babes as real call girls with a calling, the modern successors to the courtesans of legend.

I am not Phrynne, and no Canadian judge would set me free in exchange for the sight of my tits, cute as they are. But I'm not likely to get busted as long as Tom visits me at home, and neither of us has to deal with a pimp or an agency. So far, I've been able to keep my seven-year-old out of the way during his visits. With luck, she will never know about the phantom godfather who helps us survive. I guess that's why I'm grateful to him.

Tom will really owe me for this favor, and I hope he won't expect me to wear these claws every time. If I wanted to do that, I could have grown my own fingernails to a sharp and scary length with no help from gelatin. I've heard enough complaints about my own little claws, no matter how short I keep them.

I'll finish painting the ones on my left hand before I do the hand I'm using. This way, I can ease into the feeling of being manually disabled in stages. I don't feel like a tigress; *au contraire*. These things make my hands less useful, not more dangerous. I wonder if that's really why men like them.

All the men here on the alkaline prairies seem to need their gallbladders removed once they're over fifty. The minerals in the water affect everyone, but men must have more gall. It must build up in them, stagnant as swamp water. Tom expected my sympathy when he showed me his scar. I wonder if he really thinks he would like to be scratched open by a bitch in heat. I'm sure it could be done.

I can't blame the old goat for wanting to get laid, though. Everyone wants that, including me. I just don't want it with him, while he doesn't want to leave me alone, especially now that I'm trained to grease up his tool with cooking oil and suck him off the way he likes. There's the phone--it's probably him. I hope he can't come over until later.

"Jean? Are you busy?" That velvety voice is unmistakable. Whatever I say, it can't be the truth.

"Not really." This is an unforeseen disaster.

"Well, put on a pot of tea," teases the dyke of my dreams. I can hear her grinning at me over the phone. "I'm in the neighborhood, so I can come over to pick up my book if you're finished reading it. I'll be there in about ten minutes."

"Fine," I assure her, feeling faint.

"Wear something sexy," flirts Marceline. *No problem*, I think. *Your wish is granted.*

Though I suspect her concept of sexy is a little different from that of the person I am dressed for.

I don't have my act together, never did, and am very

likely to get busted after all. I should never have agreed to let my idol come here. I never know for sure when Tom will call, so he is never really out of my life. He loves his own fantasy of lesbians as hungry pussies who are always available, especially to an experienced man like him. He assumes that every dyke I know must have gentleman callers, and that I am naïve to doubt it. He wants to meet my friends. Goddess forbid.

Tom is the only man I've been seeing for over a year. He knows that, and it gives him hope that we have some kind of relationship going on. He said, "I guess you're sort of my girlfriend." I thought the "sort of" let me off the hook, so I didn't set him straight.

If anything, I am now worse than when I earned a more honest living at the agency.

There are more ways to spiral down to the depths than to get hooked on something illegal.

I can't take back my welcome because Markie (as she is known) is already on her way. She probably can't imagine what I could have to hide from her. After all, we're in the same lesbian community. We know the same people. Her girlfriend, Elaine, would probably claim to like me too, if pressed for an opinion, though that's doubtful. At this moment, Markie is probably thinking what a relief it is that none of us has to pretend to be straight in each other's company.

At this moment, I think a visit from the vice squad would be a relief.

Despite Markie's fashion advice, I have to get out of this dress before she arrives.

Luckily, it unties in a flash. Now I'm standing shamelessly in my black bra, panties, and garter belt with stockings and five-inch heels. What a spectacle for the lesbian community, if Marceline should walk in with three or four friends. I am scaring myself for no good reason.

I change into a bat-wing sweater and jeans, both comfortable but not too old. My makeup is coming off. I look as honest as I can look except for the purple claws on my left hand, which contrast with the well-clipped dykey nails on my right. I'll have to keep the claws out of sight. They are, at the very least, Politically Incorrect.

There's the doorbell. "Hi Jean," she grins, making a joke of it. The picture of health, that's me. Markie is dressed in her usual working clothes: spotlessly clean and pressed cotton pants and shirt. What else would a self-respecting lesbian-feminist wear?

Markie gives the impression of a lot of energy bursting out of a small but solid body. Her heavy breasts under a shirt manage to look motherly and butch at the same time.

"How's the zoo?" I ask her. Markie is director of the day care center in the shabby-artsy neighborhood where I live, which has been called the local Greenwich Village. She rules the staff who tend kids raised on granola and leftist righteousness. Not including mine.

"The animals have been good today," she beams. "They're making a circus mural to put up on the walls." I stand here with a whore's hand in my jeans pocket, thinking of the innocence of children. Is there no safe subject of conversation?

She is obviously wondering why we're both still standing, and why I haven't offered her anything to drink. I suspect she would accept an invitation to stay for a meal. Which might be hair pie. She could always phone Elaine with some plausible excuse.

Like royalty, Markie doesn't seem likely to leave her official consort, but I suspect that her interest in other women won't be satisfied by shallow social relationships. She has probably guessed what I want. She would probably grant my wish if it didn't cost her anything. In her supreme confidence, she probably assumes I'm just shy, or socially inept.

"Here's your book," I say brusquely, offering it with my right hand while my left stays jammed in the pocket against my hip. She reaches out with both hands, and I see that she's holding a child's drawing of a badly-proportioned woman with pointed breasts, big hair and red lips.

"See what Autumn Stormcloud made today," She laughs. "He said it's a lady on TV." She expects me to groan over the influence of patriarchal culture on impressionable young minds. She also expects me to take the drawing from her hand.

I feel faint. While my good hand pushes the book at her with unreasonable force, my left hand tries to grasp the drawing through a pocket and a thick layer of denim, which proves impossible. Markie watches me in confusion as she accepts her book.

"I'm expecting a phone call," I blurt, not wanting to lie more than absolutely necessary. "You should come over sometime when I have more time to talk." My hidden left hand forms a fist. My garters have surely left marks on my thighs like little red stigmata.

Markie's smile turns cold. "Then I won't keep you," she says. *Obviously not*, I think, *because you never had me. Probably never will, either. Especially considering the way things are going.*

My phone rings. "See you later," mouths Markie as she bounces nimbly to my door, opens it and disappears. I have no time to digest the bittersweet lost chance.

"Jean?" demands Tom in a voice that insinuates everything I have done for him, and everything else he wants but can't express in words.

"Yes," I sigh. "I'm here." He wants to come right over, so I have an indecently brief time in which to change clothes, finish applying my fake fingernails, and try to restore my makeup. I hope his own needs will distract him from noticing details.

I throw my jeans and sweater into my bedroom closet, which seems appropriate.

Back in my dress again, I look down and notice that my two hands are a study in contrast. My purple nails are no more a part of me than the heels of my shoes are part of my feet, but I agreed to wear them. The clipped nails on my right hand are useful for so many other activities. They're real and mine, but not flashy at all.

Fuck it, I think (which will soon happen in any case), *I don't have time to give myself ten phony claws like a child preparing for Halloween. He will see my face first.* So I reapply mascara and lipstick just before I hear his footsteps in the hall. He knocks quietly on my door like a criminal in a film noir. I really don't want to see Tom now, but I don't have a choice. When I open the door, I see an old vampire who feeds off the living, or a corrupt old sultan visiting a slave in his harem. I must be seeing him through Marceline's feminist eyes.

I shake my head, and see a pathetically hungry human being who has never had enough of what he wants, and whose time is running out. He wordlessly presses a wad of bills into my left hand, and I wonder if the crass nature of our relationship has come to embarrass him more than it does me. "Good to see you," he mumbles.

I try to put him at ease by explaining my good hand/bad hand dilemma. "I couldn't finish doing my nails," I tell him. "Someone I know showed up."

He smiles with fatherly generosity. "That's okay, dear. I'll wait."

This is too much. Now I owe him gratitude for letting me finish pressing on all the fake fingernails he pressed on me in the first place. He probably thinks I've become vain about my new look.

While he helps himself to coffee, I sit down to whorify my right hand. When I've finished painting the nails purple, he looks pleased. He demonstrates his pleasure by undressing in my front room and reclining on my sofa like an odalisque in a smutty Victorian painting.

I begin our usual ritual: after placing a towel under him, I drizzle oil onto his rising sausage until it gleams under my hands. My purple nails, now extra-shiny with grease, slide up and down and gently over the smooth head of an old but reliable cock. He smiles and sighs.

I lower my mouth onto him and he holds my head, running his fingers through my shoulder-length hair. I gently squeeze his balls as I lick my way over his shaft, following a familiar route. He likes what he knows.

A little scratching at the base triggers his appreciation, and my mouth is soon full of his brine. I swallow it as though it were the salty milk of disappointment. I used to insist on latex barriers for our mutual safety, but he talked me out of them years ago by telling me that he would never take such a risk with another woman, aside from his wife. I hope his pleasure is worth it. I hope I have a guardian angel.

Tom recovers enough to tell me, "You sure make my cock happy, honey." We both avoid discussing our hearts, though I know that his is threatened by high blood pressure. I wonder if his heart will ever actually break, and if this will happen while his chest is pressed to mine. I probably have nothing to gain from his death, since I doubt that my name appears in his will with those of his wife, children and grandchildren.

He wants to watch me take my clothes off. First comes the dress, which falls open as fast as a wink, then the bra that releases my small, perky breasts with nipples hardening in the air, then the stockings peeled down my legs, one at a time. I have learned to stand on one foot, and I try to strip gracefully.

Before I can pull off my panties, Tom pulls me down to lie on him. He suckles one of my nipples like a baby calf. My first reaction is revulsion; he is old enough to be my father. I can't afford to think of anything that interferes with my ability to give pleasure, though, so I close my eyes and focus on the soft, warm, insistent pull of his mouth.

I know I am becoming wet lower down. This is good, because I will soon have to welcome him into me as if I have dreamed of nothing else since his last visit.

Performing for him is a challenge every time, and I am proud that I can always do it.

He tugs at my panties. I finish pulling them off because I want to finish earning my pay. I can't help imagining his reaction if I should ever look him in the eyes and say, "I'm a whore and an actress, you fool. I've never really liked it."

Sometimes I picture an unbearably gentle look on his face as he answers, "I know, dear."

The inevitability of what is about to happen makes me wetter. I can't be sure whether pride or humility is driving him or me, but I don't want a lukewarm fuck, no matter who it's with. His fingers tease my inner lips, and slide deeper.

Tom pulls himself over me, pushing me beneath him. It's the kind of move that would look beautiful underwater, but looks faintly ridiculous on my sofa. I don't care; I spread my thighs and he plunges into my sea cave.

He pumps steadily, gaining confidence and momentum. I wonder if he enjoys me more now that I can no longer get pregnant. I had my tubes tied, partly because of him, and showed him my discreet scars after the operation.

He pulls my legs up, pressing into me. He seems happy enough. I touch his back self-consciously with my annoying fake fingernails as he rides me toward his own release.

I realize that sooner or later the long fingers of fate or time will pull us apart, and I wonder if he is worried. I can't foresee how desperately I will try to shoo him away once I have earned a graduate degree, and a teaching job appears on my horizon like the promised land. Neither of us can guess yet how hard

Tom will try to stay in my life when the time comes.

For now, my wet cunt responds to his thrusts. He grunts in a way I recognize, and I urge him on by squeezing his cock as it races to a conclusion. His relief is contagious, and I am almost honest as I fake an answering climax. I have been paid twice — in cash and in come — for my professionalism.

Thought So
Cecilia Tan

I have news for you, boys: there are horny women out there.
There are women walking the streets and bookstore aisles, or
riding trains, who are practically crying inside because they
want it so bad. Either that, or I'm the only one. But I would
put money on the fact that I am not the only one. Especially
given what Jason has told me.

It's because of Jason that I don't have to prowl those aisles,
those trains, anymore.

I first noticed him in Walpenny's, in the cookbook section.
I was thumbing through a spiral-bound volume on Thai cook-
ery when I caught him looking at me. Or maybe it was he who
caught me. By that point, I was frustrated. It was a summer
evening, cool and breezy, and though I wore a brief, swishy
dress, and had arranged my hair suggestively, I had not had
good luck. The only mild interest I'd gotten was from people I
had no interest in. And while I was starting to think I'd hump
an aardvark if I had to, I knew better.

I was biting my lip and trying to decide if I should give
up and go home, the book open in my hands but my eyes

unfocused, when Jason stepped out from behind a tall book-
case. My eyes flickered up and then back down to the book.
He was tall, a little underfed, with blue eyes and light brown
hair...and was he looking at me?

He was. I gave him a longer look, and a smile. He returned
the smile in a knowing way. *Thank goodness.* The hook was
baited. I put the book down on the table, and let my head fall
back, some of my curls brushing my bare shoulders. I saw him
gulp--hook swallowed. He came toward me and said "Hi."

"Hi," I said, lowering my eyes with a shyness that wasn't
entirely unreal. I was accustomed to being the cute one, the
desirable one--but Jason would have turned my head even if
I hadn't been having one of my horniest nights. Suddenly I
wasn't sure what to say to him.

He saved me by speaking first. "I've been following you for
a while."

"How long is a while?"

He blushed. "Since Alton Station." He reached his hand
toward mine, and brushed his fingertips against my arm. I had
to stifle an audible intake of breath. "Would you like to go
somewhere?" he asked.

I nodded. "My place, if that would be all right with you."

There was that smile again. "Lead the way." He orbited
me with a crooked arm as I turned toward the door, but he
did not touch me until we were sitting on a bench at the station. I was almost shivering by then, fantasizing about his arm
around me, waiting for it to happen--and then he slid close,
his blue-jeaned leg touching mine, and his arm slid across my
shoulders. His breath was warm in my hair, against my ear, in
the air-conditioned coolness of the station. If I had an engine,
it would have revved.

I didn't want to wait until we got home. It would be twenty
minutes on the train, and then a five-minute walk, and I was
so hot and ready that I was afraid I'd slip off the peak and lose

my edge. The frustration and need of the long evening made my jaw stiffen, the ache in my belly only intensified by the proximity of our bodies.

His lips nibbled at my ear and tears almost sprang to my eyes. He smoothed my dress down over my legs. I wished I could just lie down on the concrete bench, put up my legs and let him root around to his heart's content (and mine). Another pass with his hand.

I hadn't felt so hungrily frustrated since junior high, when I used to sit backstage during drama club rehearsal, on Daniel Pera's lap. We were too young for sex and knew it, I guess, because we never took any of our clothes off. But he used to trace every line or design on the fabric of my shirt with his fingertip, roaming featherlight over my chest and up and down my neck. Sometimes he would trace the seams of my jeans. We'd sit like that for hours, while rehearsals were going on, in the darkness of the wings, until we were needed onstage. Sometimes I went on flushed and dizzy, unsure of where my feet were, unsure even of who I was, which character I was to play, or the words I was supposed to say. I went home every night dying to masturbate the minute I got to my room.

Now Jason's fingertip began to trace the flowery vines on my dress. I shuddered a breath, in and out. I wanted to murmur sweet nothings in his ear, to give him a taste of the painful anticipation I was riding--but I could not speak. His finger slid along the center seam of my dress and came to rest at the crook of my hip. Then he turned my chin toward him, and before I could say anything, he smothered my unspoken words with a kiss.

His fingers were drumming now, like a piano arpeggio, closer and closer to where my clit throbbed under layers of clothing. Yes, I wore panties, even when out on the prowl. His gentle tapping intensified my longing. I didn't dare open my eyes, afraid that people were staring at us. He kept his rhythm even, his touch light, as if there were no urgency in him at all. The urgency was all inside me, making my shoulders tighten under his arm, my breath grow shallow, my jaw clench.

And then came the train. He held my hand and pulled me into the car. There were only four or five people within earshot, none of whom paid us any attention. Jason pulled me down into a seat and right onto his lap.

That finger of his was busy again, this time underneath my dress, pushing aside my cotton panties, then nosing back and forth through my wetness.More liquid was forthcoming, and I licked my mouth as if to match it.

When his finger slid into me, I started to cry. *You ninny*, I was thinking, *you're going to ruin it, he's going to freak and run away on you*. But I couldn't help it. His slow, gentle touch was going somewhere deep inside of me, somewhere I needed to be touched so much that the relief triggered tears. I clung to his neck and sobbed softly, my face hidden by drifts of my own hair, while his finger went in and out, soon joined by a second one. He could barely move his hand, jammed between my legs like that, but it was enough, just rocking. Then his thumb perked up and rubbed against my lubricated clit, and I sobbed harder.

"It's okay," he said into my ear. "I know."

Feeling as I had during those confused moments of stumbling from the curtains in the wings, unsure where to stand or where to go, I now found myself being carried from the train. He had me in his arms and whispered in my ear and nibbled my neck, and the next thing I knew we were at my door and he was asking for my keys. He set me down on my feet and I opened the apartment door and we climbed the dark stairs.

At the time I didn't think it odd that he knew where to go; I was too grateful to be there, mere steps from the bedroom, where we soon were, me kneeling on the bed, him standing while I unbuttoned his white cotton shirt, unbuttoned his jeans, and revealed him. His silky red erection came free and I sighed. I cupped his balls with my hand and let my lips fall around him. *Ahh. Mmm.*

He sensed that I didn't want to waste time, and let me swallow him deep a few times before he pushed forward onto the bed, flattening me in the process. We shed the rest of our clothes and I pulled a condom out of the side table drawer. I kicked off my socks while he put it on. I wrapped my legs around his back and pulled him into me.

With every thrust I felt like sparks flew down to my toes and shot out the tips of my fingers. I thought again of junior high, of a trip to the beach--baking in the sun for an hour and then running headlong down the sand and plunging into the cool water. An intensely pleasurable shock. A shockingly intense pleasure. Jason gave me that again and again.

I thrust my hips up to meet him, trying to match rhythms so as to achieve an almost violent crash of bodies. It's hard to admit this, but I wanted him to fuck me hard enough to hurt. It was one of the reasons I liked picking up strangers--they were unlikely to worry much about whether I was in pain or not. People in anonymous encounters tend to fuck with abandon. Of course, that sometimes meant that *I* would end up abandoned, if he came before me, or if he couldn't keep it up. But Jason was hanging in there, giving it to me and giving it to me.

When I'm that wet and I've wanted it for that long, I can fuck for a long, long time. I started to worry that he wouldn't last, but I didn't say anything. Just when my worrying began to distract from the pleasure, he whispered, "It's okay. I can do it." And he began to fuck even harder, and I lost myself.

The orgasm was coming--but if I followed my usual pattern, I would need a tad more clitoral stimulation. I tried to slide my hand along my stomach, but bumped into his hand, as he beat me to it. He had turned his long arm partway over and slid his thumb down over the very slippery, sensitive bump at just the right moment. Instantly, I felt the ripples build and break loose. My legs shook and my heels drummed on his back as I quaked with the power of coming. I wondered if this would make him go off, too, but when I settled back into the bed, he was still lodged deep inside me, fucking me slowly and contentedly.

Wash, rinse, repeat. After a while, he sped up, my muscles started to contract, he rubbed my clit, and--insert sound effects like Fourth of July fireworks. And again. And maybe again...I can't do math when I'm like that. I kept thinking, *Oh, this time he'll go off, too.* But he didn't. And then I started to feel like I'd had enough and I feared that he hadn't, and I was going to end up having to go through the ordeal of letting him fuck me when I didn't want to anymore. It would not be fair, after all, to get what I wanted and leave him unsatisfied.

Suddenly he pulled out, lay back next to me, and smiled.

"You didn't come," I said.

"Are you sure?" he asked.

"Yes." I put my hand on his chest and felt his heart beating hard. "I'm sure of it."

"You're right."

"Do you want me to go down on you?" I could not move at that point, as I lay there, thoroughly screwed, but I figured I'd be able to sit up in a few minutes.

"No, that's okay," he said, sounding sleepy, or maybe I was projecting. "You just rest."

We lay there in the semidarkness of the streetlight, and after a short nap, my brain began to perk up. That's when I realized that I had never told him where I lived, nor how to get there. He had been following me all evening, by his own admission. I didn't think I would feel so comfortable snuggling up to a psycho. Did I have a stalker?

"No," he said, stroking my hair. "I can read your mind."

"What do you mean, you can read my mind?" I guess I thought it was some mushy romantic thing he was trying to say. But I was wrong. He meant it in the most literal sense.

"In the bookstore, you picked up that cookbook because you thought the cover image looked phallic."

"Spring rolls and bananas."

"Then you watched that clerk, the one with the nose ring, walk by, and decided you really didn't like the way he smelled." His voice was soothing. "That's the smell of patchouli, by the way."

"And what was I thinking about when we were in the train station?"

The Man Who Came To Dinner."

"Holy shit." That was the play we'd done in drama club. He really could read my mind. "So you were following me around all night, and knew how horny I was the whole time?"

"Yes."

I propped myself up on an elbow and slapped him on the shoulder. "That's for making me wait so long." Then I kissed him, long and deep, until we were both breathless.

He started to get up and I thought, *Aha, now he'll want to come.* But he made a quick trip to the bathroom, and when he returned, began to get dressed.

I asked him if he wanted to come and he smiled that sweet smile at me. "Yes, very much. But I'm going to wait."

I wasn't sure what to think about that. "Why?"

"You wanted me to experience the exquisite pain you had gone through. I figured I'd try it." He leaned over and kissed me on the lips, then again on the forehead. It struck me then that I couldn't just let him walk away, like any other anonymous encounter. "Will you come back tomorrow?"

"If you want me to."

"You have to." I told him I wouldn't feel complete until he came, too.

And he said: "I know."

Man and Woman:
A Study in Black and White
Rachel Resnick

She was meeting a gorgeous black man she'd recently and violently fallen in love with, and the obsession was at full throttle. As she waited, she worried about not looking good enough for him. When she stood, this angular, show-stopping redhead with the frantic green orbs, she was painfully aware of the new garter belt slipping from her waist and the garters themselves poking into the excess fat of her thighs. He liked it when girls went without underwear, so she'd purchased this garter-hose ensemble, not expecting the discomfort of her nether lips chafing together as she walked or the chill that would rise from beneath her filmy skirt and strike her where the soreness began; after she came under the expert ministrations of his tongue, he liked to jam his fingers deep inside her to make her scream, only she never did. Instead, her vaginal walls were raw and bruised. She secretly delighted in the sensation, a forget-me-not etched into flesh, proof of his desire. She had worried about indulging her fetish for blacks, reminding herself that she was always falling in love and had proved herself incapable of having casual sex even with men she didn't fancy, but she was resolved that this time would be different. This time she would be in control. He would be her fantasy stud, her own Ray Victory, starring with her in a new make-believe segment of her favorite porn video, *Black Ass/White Gash*. She watched this video frequently. It had choreographed her masturbatory sessions for some years now, though none of her terminally PC friends knew. And it prepared her for the real weekend he and she had spent together, the one when she vowed she'd keep it about raw sex and not trip out on the man; in less than a week, though, her plans had disintegrated.

Even the way she stood on the Promenade, leaning against the glass of a light fixture store, seemed awkward, and she couldn't manage to arrange her legs properly. What stupidly long legs! They were hopeless. Her skin was so pale it was almost see-through. She may as well be wrapped in rice paper. She saw a thick throbbing purple vein on the back of her hand she'd never seen before. Were her organs showing through? But no, her skin was more like coagulated glue—opaque, and pasty. A canvas for freckles and sunspots, veins and scratches. She hated pale with a passion. If only she could go out in the sun without turning into a tomato face. The zipper on the skirt was puckering; why hadn't she noticed earlier? Thoughts were ping-ponging around her head, zigzagging the heart chakra. Her belly pooched under the tight black stretch top, and she was sure she hadn't covered up the spots on her face where she'd been picking and prodding at acne. At her age (she was twenty-nine—OK, thirty-three—to his twenty-four) she shouldn't be getting acne anymore and she should know better than to pick, but then, if he could mark her, why shouldn't she mark herself as well? It was a week since they'd first met and spent a whole torrid weekend together, and she hadn't heard one peep from him until a few hours ago when he'd called her at the office to ask her out, and she'd said sure, she'd meet him for a movie later—then she'd freaked, realizing it was Friday afternoon and she was a chump for saying she was available. Why would a stud like him want to fuck with a pale, neurotic girl like her anyway? Correction: an "older woman," as he'd said (without even knowing her correct age!). He was probably not going to show, or he was going to dump her in some humiliating fashion, and it would be nobody's fault but her own. She was close to despair about its being over, so she'd stopped at a bar beforehand and had a few espressos along with a couple of shots of Jack, which only contributed to her sense of fragmentation.

He was late. Perhaps he wouldn't show. Miserable, she wandered into a trendy clothing store and was instantly mesmerized by the gaudy displays, the raucous derangement of cheap finery. Everything seemed to vibrate in the anticipation of his arrival. Absently she ran her fingers through a rack of silken blouses, and thought of his skin, its ebony perfection, turning away when an anorexic salesgirl wearing a hoodie top and yellow-tinted aviators moved toward her with predatory speed. When was it she'd first understood her craving for black skin? Was it when she read To Kill a Mockingbird as a child, and sensed that behind the chifforobe, it was really about fear of black men's virility, and if there was that much fear, there must be something fearsome to back it up? Was it her childhood in Podunk, Florida, where she'd fantasized about the ripped blacks who ran track so effortlessly, who seemed to go airborne on the basketball court, who danced with a feral grace and moved through the cinderblock halls with warrior strides and whose physiques put the crackers to shame, and who either would look through her as if she was invisible when she made eyes at them, or would say nasty, vulgar things to her at the lockers—either way, they were so close she could taste their sweat, see their muscles shifting underneath their skin, but never touch them. They were completely out of reach. Tantalizing and taboo. Maybe it dated to the first time she'd heard Jimi Hendrix as a kid, and throughlined into her lifelong predilection for sappy black pop. In the music, as in their presence, she maintained that black men were more rooted in their sexuality than white men, more confident, more attuned. Maybe it had something to do with the scalding memory of certain rednecks who jokingly dared each other, "Nickel for every nigger you hit," in the school parking lot, flooring their Camaros and pickups past the blacks who, too poor to own cars, were walking home to the projects. But until she met him (he was a purebred, African blood to the core, while she was a typical Made-in-America Euro mutt; white trash, to her own mind) she'd never actually slept with one. Sleeping with him, and having it surpass the most explosive orgasms she'd had during sessions with her trusty *Black Ass/ White Gash* tape and Dutch, the ten-inch cyberskin motorized dildo, had soldered her preconceptions. Now a silk shirt with a hula girl motif was in her hands, and she held it before her dreamily, seeing the shirt enshrining him. She was hopelessly snared, and she thought of the African tale retold by Amos Tutuola, about a man who meets a woman in Africa at the market, and he invites her home to visit. He is the Perfect Gentleman, handsome and courteous and kind. She follows him. Along the way he begins taking off his clothes, dropping them behind. Then he starts removing his limbs. Arms. Legs. Torso. Until he is nothing but a skull bouncing along the dirt road. Because she wears the cowrie shell necklace he gave her, she is under his spell and must keep following him. Where would he lead her? What was he taking, and what would he give back? The stupid saying *Once you go black, you never go back* kept cycling through her fevered brain. No wonder most people clamped the sewer grate down on their own subterranean appetites. She saw a dark clotted river of Lethe in an underground subway, choked with shit and crawling with blink-eyed albino alligators, and shuddered. She returned the shirt to the rack. After all, he was Jamaican. African by way of the Caribbean. Hula girls made no sense.

The pulse of fluorescence and the oiled sweetness of an old Johnny Gill tune that came on the radio spurred a vision from last weekend of them lying entangled there on her bed, his buttery blackness draped over the white of her. Checkerboard girl. "I love you more than I've ever loved anyone. I want to do things to you I've never done to anyone else," she imagined him saying, though he had said nothing of the sort. Instead, he had charmed her with his growling and purring as he fucked her so deep down and rough she still ached. In the picture she conjured up, she marveled at how his ebony body contrasted with the whiteness of her and gave it buoyancy, density, almost beauty—as if she were an unfinished sketch of blank space, and he shaded her in. As she sank into reverie, her groin inflamed and her chest palpitated. She knew the vision was a cheesy BET video, sentimental, maybe reverse racist, but she couldn't help it. The heat was on. When she'd first learned of her appetite for black men, she'd understood what it was to look at sexuality like a stranger, the stranger within, but one who must be greeted and welcomed. Move over, Ray Victory. This Jamaican was her dream man. If she weren't in Los Angeles, so far from family, she never would have had the guts. Lucky she'd gone to that stupid VIP nightclub party. She'd seen him and thought, no way can he be straight; he was too breathtaking, stylish, in shape. Before they even spoke, he'd taken her out on the dance floor and led her in a sexy slow dance grind, ending with a dip! and she'd changed her mind. Even more serendipitous that he'd been there at all, since blacks and whites, as well as other ethnicities, were more segregated in L.A. than back home. Now, the thought of losing him struck her with a panic. The world seemed suddenly flushed with bright white, starchy with unhealth and imminent collapse, and lacking the grace of salvation. Even the mannequins looked startled at their loss of innocence. That same salesgirl, her aviators now accusingly yellow, clopped toward her, bearing down.

She exited the clothing store, kneading her hands to slow down the nerves. From somewhere came the smell of fresh caramel corn, so sweet it was sickening. She tugged nervously at her hose, thinking they had slid around her thighs, and clutched her jacket about her. The sky was gray and drained of all color, and she wondered if she could survive such a need. Which is when she saw him coming around the corner and immediately creamed.

He was dressed casually, but self-consciously. Studied cool. She'd noticed last weekend that he seemed to be a bit of a control freak, given to extra hand-washing and a certain fastidiousness, especially with food—only tofu for him. In a way, his pickiness and concern about weight reminded her of a woman. Perhaps that was part of the allure, too. Tonight he wore an expensive white T-shirt that hugged his sculpted chest and shoulders, a pair of worn jeans (what were called "date rape" pants) with holes in the ass and knees, fashionably baggy, but cinched at the waist with a black bandana for a belt. Black clogs. A leather jacket. Hair in shoulder-length dreads. Striking face with that pure, flattish African nose and flared nostrils, lively dark brown eyes, lush mouth. No jewelry. Didn't matter. He could've worn anything and stopped traffic. When he walked, the slight bow in his ballet legs was exaggerated, another sexy trait. Only a dancer could get away with clogs. She wondered again briefly if he was gay somewhere under there. Weren't they all? Meaning, all men. Women were just shadows to them, things to catch and break, to penetrate and impregnate, whereas other men were meat and muscle, car talk and jock walk. Solid. Simple. Familiar. He was terribly late, but walked nonchalantly toward her, and though she knew she should be insulted, she could not help smiling. She pictured him in his Calvins. He had been an underwear model in Japan. Once, he had told her, during a nude photo shoot for a fashion mag, a model who had been lying on top of him during a complicated shot left a wet mark. "Your abs," she whispered. "I've never seen anything like them." He got a huge boner and had to excuse himself to go to the bathroom. The Japanese stared, mouths open.

"*Bonsoir, chérie,*" he said, but he seemed distracted and mouthed the words as if he relished the sound of his mush-mouthed French accent more than the meaning, or the impact. She herself, a highly successful entrepreneur and certifiable workaholic, had never yet been to Paris, whereas he had done photo shoots and gone on a tour with his dance troupe there. Now, after a mysterious injury, he was retired from dancing and worked as a bartender at a posh Beverly Hills watering hole. As for modeling, he said he didn't like being stared at that way, like an object. Not that she cared about any of that. She had money enough for both of them, though he always insisted on paying his half. Why was he was so spacey? Had he just come from seeing someone else? Although she impulsively went to hug him and kiss him on the lips, he hesitated, as if he'd blanked out on the whole greeting ritual—or, worse, forgotten who she was. Maybe she was being overly pushy, even hokey, and he preferred a cooler public demeanor? Her right eyelid began to twitch, very slightly, and she hoped he wouldn't notice. Did he see her shoes?

"Hey," she said. Trying to be laidback, not mentioning the time. Wondering if he was hard.

"Check the shoes. Cute." He paused, long enough for her to fall into compliment quicksand, where she was still pleasantly sinking when he followed with, "Why so dressed up, girl?"

She felt the blush. Instant tomato face. Why did she think of a one-two combination? Hook-jab-jab. She looked at his face and wondered if she was only imagining that he looked somehow pleased with himself, pleased with hurting her, but at that instant he grabbed her arm and she spun out, dizzy with the sensation. If he asked her, she would drop to her knees and suck him off right there. Let all Santa Monica watch. *Melting, I'm melting,* flashed in her brain, and the witchy striped socks hissed and curled away.

"I want to be your slave," she heard herself say from far away.

"Speak up, girlfriend."

"I will be your slave."

He looked at her then, more intently. The corners of his thick-lipped mouth turned up slightly, like pan-fry fish that is just beginning to burn.

At the doorway to her canyon house, she had forgotten to flip the outside light, and it was swamped in inky canyon night. His hand was electrifying her hip, but when she craned around she could hardly see him; his skin was the night air. A fat yellow moth stuttered drunkenly toward the light, and bumped smack against the bulb. She thought she heard a wing fry as the light singed it. Tsss. Then he smiled, and each gleaming tooth acted as a cowrie shell, binding her to his will. She faced the door now, bending slightly so that her hips and ass would move into his groin. So that she could press against his hardness. As she turned the key in the lock, he reached his hand up under her skirt, between her legs. She heard him draw in his breath, but kept on with the key. The lock clicked. The door opened. He smeared her juice slowly on the inner thigh and gently withdrew his hand.

"Good girl," he said.

Then he was guiding her through the doorway, surrounding her like a cape, kissing her ear. The way his tongue scoured the cochlea, setting the eardrum to pounding, each lapping released another cunt wave. If this ear were a fig, she would

want all the fruit flesh tongued out until she was deaf to everything but the sound of him. As her cunt flared in anticipation,
she tugged at his springing dreads. He pulled back slightly and
she panicked.

"I'm taking my time," he said into her ear. His tongue
puddled deeper as her nipples strained to pop through the
crisp lace of her costly bra. Black. Yes, of course. Gothic
against her pallor. Lingerie as contrast. Enticement's in the
eye of...sweet Jesus....

But then he withdrew his tongue and pushed her so that she
stumbled, and clattered to the floor. Déjà vu. Was she dreaming
this or was someone videotaping? She looked at her hand
splayed on the cold Italian tile to see if it was a grainy video
hand, but no. Who was directing? He pulled his T-shirt over
his head and it was gone. There he was. She couldn't breathe.
Could not. It would've been enough to simply stare, pray to
that body, the arc of pectoral triumph, baby-smooth sable
skin, physique's articulation of the perfect mean, the golden
triangle, the hypotenuse of her desire for African splendor.

"Fold my shirt," he said. "Bitch."

Actually, he didn't say "bitch" but she wished he had. His
mother had raised him strict backwoods Christian, island-
style, and he had trouble with swearing, though not with
fucking, thank the gods. This mother of his was partial to the
switch, or cook pot, or hand, whatever was easiest. Besides
the beatings, she'd also enjoyed dressing him up, more than
her daughters. He was the cute one. There was no question he
had a dark well to draw from in the sexual arena. And she'd
been encouraging from the start, telling him *no limits*. She
wondered where it would take her, and him. How could he
not fall for her? Wasn't she liberating him?

Swooning with longing, with lust, she crawled to the pile
of shirt, kissed it first, (what was she doing?), shook it out,
and made it into a tight little square, like they do with shirts

in plastic packages (how did she know how to do that?). Then her hair was in his hand, being twisted, and he was leading her to the bathroom. Better than she could've imagined.

"Clean my ass."

What? He was really coming into his own. She thought of the scene in the video where Ray Victory shaves this white chick's legs with a cheap Bic razor and shaving cream while they're sitting naked in a tub in an empty House for Sale. The slap and slosh of water, and soap, and skin, his black arm moving down her perky leg...but before she could fast-forward to the good stuff, his hand on her bony but shapely ass returned her to now time. In her charming three-quarter-million-dollar canyon house, not a rinky-dink porn set. Everything red under a weird heat light, giving his impossibly smooth skin a devil sheen, and him handing her a wad of toilet tissue. Then a washcloth he'd dampened under warm water, and offered, moist, soapy. Single, antichildren, and addicted to maid service, she'd never even cleaned a baby's bottom, nor changed a diaper, nor taken a shit with someone else in the bathroom, nor on their chest even when they asked her to—sometimes there were limits. But not now. Not in now time. In the red zone. With this vision before her, this Jamaican hunk, who needed, who wanted, his ass cleaned. So be it.

Swabbing the black ass bathed in red glow as he leaned against the marble scallop sink, she who never even cleaned her house, nor swiped a counter, was in heaven. Squeezing one rocky muscular buttock while she rubbed the cloth in circular motions over his anus, gingerly pressing and working a corner into the hole and wiggling her finger there. But he tensed and her finger was ejected. Drawing the damp cloth slowly down to cup his balls as she involuntarily went for the other virgin ass cheek and kissed, and bit. Insane with need. Then traced a finger over that cheek. Worshipfully. Until her finger reached the rectal starburst, and stopped in wonder at the extraordinary lips she found there. Forming a perfect O. This was not her thing. No way. But impulsively, she moved toward the circular puckered flesh and began kissing those still slightly acrid lips, and tonguing, and licking, taking the flaps of anal flesh into her mouth, being careful not to bare any teeth. With the other hand she flicked the halogen on and gasped at the succulence of black ass before her as the bright light defined it.

He growled. Swiveling his ass. No one's mouth had ever entranced her so much.

He purred. With her other hand she reached up between the taut dancer legs and grabbed only the root of his cock. And squeezed, in time with her mouth's lapping, and felt the blood rush there, swelling, and imagined it coursing thick and red-black through the ridged and lovely veins. Give her a century, folded into a parcel of time, and she would spend it like this. Pleasing him. Then, keeping her right hand on his cock's base, and her mouth paying attention to his asshole, she moved her left hand between her own legs and dipped in a finger to see how wet she was, and could not believe it.

"Don't forget your own, dirty girl. Wash up good."

Keeping her hand on his cock, working it to the middle, squeezing, then to the top, right under the flared mushrooming uncircumcised head, squeezing, feeling the cock grow bigger—she rinsed the washcloth under the running spigot, and dabbed at her own still-sore asshole, and at her cunt, though the pressure was almost too much, she was so aroused. If he had not then risen up, circled her throat with his chocolate-black fingers, and pressed, and raised her up, and moved her before him as they glided into the master bedroom, she would've come just from the intimate worship he was demanding, and allowing. Gone was the girl in him. Only the warrior prince of lovemaking remained.

He picked her up then, and tossed her onto the bed. She

understood. Just the skirt came off. Spiky heels dug into the mattress, her garters scraped, and her swollen pussy lay open to the world. Which was him. There he was, standing there looking down on her, his fantastic ten-inch (ten-foot?) cock arching and jerking on its own, making little stuttering probes into the air. Somehow he was completely and stunningly naked. The whites of his eyes shone; his body was mythical. As he looked at her she knew to spread her legs and slowly part the sopping lips with her fingers, showing what color she had, offering him the pink, and he took it. He descended onto the bed, her body—this black Adonis—and buried his head between her legs. After some minutes of licking her gently around the pulsating mound, making her mad with lust and impatience, sending more juices spooling onto the sheets, he sat up and wound a plastic key coil from his wrist around his dreads so that they were gathered into a topknot, giving him a deliciously androgynous touch. Too sexy. Too much. Those bee-stung lips on her cunt lips, pulling and sucking, teasing the clit, soon sent spirals and circles, sunbursts and ricochets of almost psychedelic sensation ribboning through her body.

"Fingers," she breathed.

"Don't rush me," he said sharply. Hovering on the edge of orgasm, she didn't register the harshness. The contrast with his skill. Was he not giving her mind-blowing pleasure? With her own fingers, she twisted both her nipples, amped up the thrill. Then she pinched until they stood up like rosy peaks of meringue. He saw her, briefly reached up and cupped one of her small but supple breasts. Finally he entered a finger in her cunt. Her strong muscles immediately closed around the digit. Then a second. He reached her G-spot right away, as if by radar. Or, was it love? Was it? Soul mates? Wouldn't that make everyone crazy? She closed her eyes. As he kept licking her lips and clit, he pounded his fingers against the G-spot, so she had to keep zoning toward that place where she was approaching orgasmo light, then backing off because there was now too much sensation.

Then she couldn't hold back. She saw herself, supine, red hair matted and spread like a banquet around her head, green eyes glazed, long milky-white limbs, cream-white skin, spinning around the smoky-black pivot of him, like paints are spun in metal bowls and splatter onto paper, creating fantastical random designs. Things telescoped, got larger, then smaller. She was an elephant. She was Thumbelina.

"You're raining on me," he said, in awe. At their bond? At his skill? Holding one hand under her to catch the wetness as he continued ramming his fingers against her G-spot. At first this extra sensation added texture to the orgasm; then it became painful. She wriggled to get away, scooching up the mattress, but she cracked her skull against the wall. He rammed harder. Furiously. His breath grew shallow. He seemed unaware of her, unstoppable. It was then she remembered she was on the tail end of her period. Probably it was all gone, but there was a chance deep inside there was still some blood. She worried it might bother him, anal as he was, but dared not interrupt him now. The pain mounted, but he kept going, and going, until he was done. She realized then, as she concentrated on the awful stabbing in her cunt, that as hard as he'd made her come, he only stopped when he'd had enough, not when she had. There was an important message there, but she was not quite able to grasp it, sex-drunk as she was.

An aromatherapy Passion candle flickered suddenly, then guttered. Others danced and flickered wild, shaggy shadows against the walls. A stick of Nag Champa incense burned in the corner, dropping ash as it kept trying to reach the ceiling. Gypsy fabrics hung over expensive tabletops, and Tiffany lampshades. So Topanga. He had opened her up and she could do nothing but wait to be filled, when and if he chose. The candlelight was low; she hoped he hadn't noticed any red on his fingers. With luck it was all gone. In the shifting glow of flame, his topknot looked regal.

"God, I love your dreads," she said with a sigh and tried to reach toward him.

"You know," he said, sitting up abruptly, stroking his licorice-black cock, his eyes shiny and sharp, "where I come from, it is not Kingston. In the hills of Jamaica live the Wharricks, my family. We are descended from slaves, but we escaped. It was the 1700s and the Spanish were there, then the British. They call us Maroons. And they say my family is descended from Grandy Nanny, who led the escape. She wore branches in her hair and they believed nothing could touch her. People don't understand. They ask me about these dreads. They call me 'Bob Marley.' I have never smoked ganja. I do not listen to reggae. My family is all preachers. Do you know what I am saying?"

She didn't have time to wonder at his strange monologue, to substitute endearments for his words, or even to respond. Instead he pulled her toward him and slid his cock unceremoniously into her slippery cunt. Time stopped. Clocks broke. Skies fell. Rivers rose. Trees walked. Time was now split. There was time before his cock penetrated, and after. Before, when things were black and white, and after, when things were Technicolor.

"Nice and hot," he said about her twat—his words, again, not matching her thoughts or mood. Not that she noticed, really.

The thrusting was brutal. Banging against all manner of vaginal stalagmites and bumps and hidden chambers. She grabbed at his sculpted shoulders, urging him deeper. Subsumed the pain. Pain on pain, producing pleasure. She raised her womanly hips, braced her hands against the walls, contorted herself to take him all the way. I'm not your girl, I'm your gash. That's all. Slit. Slash. Gash. White gash. Got it? Take me. Take all I have, then I will have you. She was a wound waiting to be opened. Red underlines white, clashes with black. No, she didn't think it mattered, the very slight chance of remaining menstrual blood. But might it? With such a man, so clean. So newly clean.

"I'm almost done with my period," she whispered. Hoarsely. In case there was a last trace left. And to her horror, with only one quick grunt, he stopped. For a moment, an instant, he was inside her, not moving. He would stay there, wouldn't he? He understood he was home? Together they made home? But then there was a sucking, slurping pop, and he was out, and her cunt collapsed along with her heart. Kerthump.

"Ras clot," he said. And she could barely understand. The Jamaican patois.

"Bumba clot. Ras clot," he said. Again. This time she got it. Blood clot. Right. Shit. He'd told her about this last weekend, this Jamaican paranoia for menstrual blood. Shit. Blood clot was the biggest insult you could use on a Jamaican. It meant that something like you came out of your mother's womb as a blood clot, not as an ovum? Or did it mean you were a blood-soiled period rag? Whatever. It was bad. No point in explaining now how she was just being extra careful.

Then, still leaning over her, facing her, he grabbed for her ass. Her ragged, sore ass. Clean, yes. Bloodless, true. She cringed. Last weekend, one brutish time, had been enough. She'd fantasized about it, yes, she'd egged him on, but the truth was it had hurt like hell. Now he nosed his massive cock at her hole like some kind of shit-skin flesh missile, then shoved. All the way. Involuntarily, she cried out, "No!," forgetting her promise to him, her need. Didn't he know about lubricant? Or was he unleashing some demon? He began pounding hard and deep; she could feel his cock swelling even larger. Impossible that she could even take him. She kept crying out, stuff she didn't even clock. "Please, oh, no, stop. It hurts. No..." but he paid no attention; thrust harder. She thought of a multitude rowing somewhere they didn't want to go, plowing through a jet-black sea, rowing bodies that were stretched to the limit, until their muscles began snapping like rubber bands, shooting all over the ship's murky bowels, and he came, shuddering over her. There he was, her merciless ebony god, arching his glorious back, his eyes rolled back in his head, his topknot shaking like spongy twigs as he threw his head back and stretched his arms out to the sides as if he were welcoming his own mysterious god. It struck her then, as she lay ravaged, sober now, blood leaking from her torn asshole, pinpricks of pain throbbing in her rectum, watching his unseeing eyes, the smug satisfaction in his beauty, in his prowess, that this was all about him. She was merely a sacrifice. A white girl gift. A boon to his path toward sadism. Toward ownership. Perhaps toward retribution. This was not love. She, the fetishizer, was being fetishized! He was tripping on the pliancy, the devotion, of someone who worshiped him, Black Stud. He was checked out. Unconnected. Dominant. By fetishizing the fetishizer, he'd turned the tables. While she herself had broken the cardinal rule of objectifying: She'd made her Jamaican fuck stud into a beloved man and so lost all power. So she thought. But her cunt was still sloppily, slap-happily swimming in that inky black sea. Blissful. Wasn't that what it was all about? The heart is not so easy to harness.

He was still hard. Would he return to her? She pulled him closer, with elegant, spidery, pearly-white fingers. Probing for a weak spot.

"What's a little teeny bit of blood, if there even is any?" she whispered, overcome by her own need. Balance the ugliness with the primal merging she loved best, his fudge-black cock melting in the ice-cream dream of her white gash. Cajoling. "I mean, I'm bleeding now from my butt...."

He shook his head. "Nuh the same." And shuddered by way of explanation. Christ on a stick, she thought.

"C'mon, you're a stud. Blood can be hot. One time this guy, he went down on me when I was bleeding buckets. His face was smeared with blood. It was beautiful."

Silence sank over their tangled black-and-white bodies, like an invisible mosquito net, sank into the sweat- and come- and juice-soaked mattress, knitting everything together.

"Please?" Blushing that her voice had so betrayed her, softly cracking.

She was shocked when he began moaning. Had she turned him on? Seduced him with her plea? A smile played across her full lips. But when she reached down, the magnificent cock had dwindled to a soft wrinkled thumb, and now, what was this? He was curling, hunching, into a fetal position, moving himself into the warping shape of her, and his toned flanks shook. Was he trembling? Shaking. Quaking. She thought of a party balloon, overinflated to that dangerous tautness, shiny in its thin state—then the flatulent hiss as the balloon was released and scudded around the room until it landed there, in the dust, wet and darker and deflated.

"What're you doing to me?" he said, burying his head between her tiny breasts. "Mi nuh wan de ras clot."

"OK. Roger. 10-4," she said, giving up. Giving up on the syrupy love dream she'd poured over the original checkerboard fantasy. Clearly they were each orbiting in their own horny worlds with their own gods and monsters. Owning didn't figure in. Neither did love. Did they? She needed to get grounded again, plant her snow-white feet back in the brown-black earth. Amazingly, he was already out. Lightly snoring.

With one ivory-white hand she clicked on the VCR, to the part in the tape where Ray Victory shaves whitey chick's pussy clean, with short, even, raspy strokes, dipping that Bic in the tub water, sudsing her cunt, taking his time, being thorough, and then he's done; he sets down the razor, there's a splashing as he rises up from the bathtub edge, facing her, moving toward her, parting those tub waters toward this dimpled white trash gash, placing his dark hands so firmly on either pale hip, giving them meaning, giving them definition, and finally, finally—watch how that mud-black cock goes in so smooth, that elegant inky snake entering the shaved white lips, parting them and feeding them what they've been needing, and finally he's wet-slapping his big black cock into and against her wet white flanks. Look at her dimples, her mouth an ecstatic O. Even she is surprised by just how big it is once inside her, that shadow man unleashed; look at her straining to hold herself steady against the faux-rock wall as he pumps her, drills her, shows her who's the man, who's the master, who's holding all history's cards....

...And with her other bone-white hand, now completely translucent in the unearthly glow from the TV, our enlightened redhead first stroked the springy dreads of her trembling black stud, then reached her hand under the covers and stroked her honky-tonk pussy.

Memories
Barbara Roduner

"Of course they'll get back together," I said, stepping off the bus after my sister.

"Of course they *won't*," she shot back. At fifteen she was two years older and smarter, and far too eager to wound a sister who was already aching.

"Will too," I retorted, convinced I was right. "Mom and Dad love each other. It's just another argument. You'll see. Everything will be fine."

"Have it your way; I'm going down to Judy's," she said with that 'you are the stupidest person in the world' look.

She has to be wrong, I thought, watching her trudge through the spring afternoon, heavy schoolbooks weighing her down.

As her figure retreated, I glanced up the hill toward our house, an unhappy place to live in for years now. Unhappiness got to you, crept inside you, lived there if you let it, so I'd forced mine out, telling myself over and over again, *Everything will be fine.*

I swallowed, looking up at that house, because somehow,

today, everything didn't *look* fine. Sighing at what a twerp I was, I straightened my heavy pile of books and started up the hill, wondering why everything was so quiet.

It was Wednesday, the one day that my father, being a doctor, could be anywhere. Mom had been staying with Gram for over a month—ever since a horrid fistfight with Dad. But she was due home this weekend and I could hardly wait. Once she was home everything would be fine. Just fine. My sister would see.

Suddenly I looked up in surprise. The front door should be open. It always was—flung wide after my two rambunctious brothers barged through. I had come to appreciate that wide-open door; I enjoyed being able to walk right in with my heavy books.

I balanced my books on my hip and tried the door. It was locked. I got a funny, prickly kind of feeling running up my spine. What was going on? The front door was never locked.

I rebalanced all my books, walked down the top part of the circular drive, around the flower beds, and then up the drive-way to the back entrance. The garage door was down; the garage door was *never* down. I felt weirder and weirder.

As I set my books on the milk box, I was surprised to find myself sweating. I shrugged and opened the screen door. Mounting the four shallow steps to the rear entrance, I found what I'd never doubted—the *back* door was locked.

There were no windows in the garage door, but there was a side window to the garage itself. Long ago, Mom had shown me where the extra house key was. I collected it and peeked through the side window. Sure enough, there was Dad's Lincoln Continental.

I was so nervous I could barely fit the key in the lock as I held the screen door open with my tush, a screen door that still had the glass in it because my mother hadn't been there to see that it was changed. Finally the key fit the lock and turned properly and I was in. But what was I in *to*? It seemed overly warm after the crispness of outside, and dark, too.

I looked around, trying to accustom myself to the dimness as I took off my jacket and listened. Was that giggling? *Giggling*? Afraid for my precious books, I brought them in and laid them on the kitchen counter next to my jacket.

That *was* giggling! It was a woman's voice—not my mother's—joined by a lower male voice, definitely my father's. I sat down on the kitchen floor, not sure what to do. I was horrified and angry all at once.

As my eyes grew used to the dimness, I saw various items of clothing scattered around the kitchen. A stiletto high heel, trousers, a silk stocking, a pair of expensive men's shoes, and over by the dining room a monogrammed silk shirt.

I stared and stared at that shirt, knowing that the dining room just beyond held a secret—if I could only think of it. Then I remembered. I remembered that little window—the one the help always used to pass hors d'oeuvre trays through at parties.

I could use it to see just what dear old Dad was up to. Up to without shoes or trousers or shirt. With a giggling woman with no skirt or blouse, a lone silk stocking, and one stiletto high heel.

I'd always known my father couldn't keep his *putz* in his pants--known it instinctively, and known it from my mother's mouth. But until I silently slid that serving window up, not actually seeing it had saved my heart.

Still, the scene before me took me unawares, as if I'd had no idea what to expect. Shivering, I froze, my mind turning cool and detached as I silently viewed the startling sight.

They lay entwined on the couch, her ruby-red lipstick all over his lips and cheek. She'd obviously kissed him many times, while I'd been serenely riding the bus home from school.

They were both vain: my father dyed his forty-year-old

head of hair black, and she'd bleached hers platinum. The woman giggled, murmuring, "Uhm, Mel," as he pushed aside the lace of her heavily-padded bra and licked her nipple.

So odd to see your father making love to a strange woman. Very odd indeed. Scary--and tingly too.

I studied her figure. Not as good as Mom's. Little tits and a big ass. Still, Dad seemed to like her body. Liked it a lot, judging from the noises he made.

Somewhere along the line Dad must have shed his socks because he sure wasn't wearing them now--just an undershirt and boxers. Mom had always wanted him to wear briefs because they "looked neater," but *doctor* Dad refused to have his "sperm restricted."

Sperm restricted. I suddenly realized I knew a lot of medical terms. "You're so lucky to have a doctor for a father," my friends would say.

Was I lucky? I felt edgy and weepy because I didn't know the answer. Lucky? Maybe. All I knew was my home was a mess and I was one big aching hole.

Dad slipped the shoulder straps of her bra down, his hands and fingers lingering over the heavy flesh of her arms, and then I heard her name for the first time.

"Lara," he breathed.

Lara—a name that would change my life forever. He lingered over her name just as he'd lingered over her clinging flesh.

Silent as a cat, I grabbed a dining-room chair. This was going to take time and I was going to be comfortable. My fingers brushed against my breast as I positioned the expensive Chippendale; I was stunned to find my nipple sensitive and hard as a rock.

"Mel?" came a frightened bit of sound. "Did you hear something?"

"Don't worry, honey, everything's locked up tight as a

drum," Dad reassured as I peeked out at them carefully. "The girls are visiting friends and the boys are with their mother."

There was something about the way he said "their mother" that I didn't like. Something scathing and filled with loathing.

"She'll go through with it, won't she, Mel?" this Lara asked.

"She'd better," Dad said, his voice low and bitter. What in hell was he talking about?

I watched curiously as my father took a long suck at the woman's nipple, fully visible for the first time. My eyes popped in amazement: her nipple was huge and *brown*. I hadn't known there *were* brown nipples.

Lara had tiny little hands and she smiled as she worked them under my father's T-shirt. He favored those athletic, tank-top kind, not the neat crew necks my mother liked.

My brow suddenly furrowed as I realized that when my father liked hot my mother liked cold. I squirmed in my seat, trying to shake off the heavy sense of foreboding that came with that thought, but it didn't work.

"You look sexy in this," Lara purred, breaking in on my disturbing thoughts.

Her tiny hands rubbed and teased my father's chest, his breath growing rough and labored until, little by little, those small hands worked off a T-shirt my mother despised.

My eyes grew wide, for there was my father's chest. One solid mass of black hair. I'd seen him at the beach. Why hadn't I noticed?

"Let's make a fire," Lara suddenly invited, filled with enthusiasm. My father blinked, obviously drawn back from a place so sexually enticing that he didn't want to leave.

"First take the edge off," Dad winked. This couldn't be the first time for these two, and Lara wasn't, as I'd hoped, a rented prostitute or floozy pickup. Dad cared about this woman. This was dangerous.

"My, my, Dr. Verlaine, just how would I go about doing such a thing?" the woman who was neither a prostitute nor a floozy asked, her fingers swirling within the slit of his boxers.

"My dear Miss Martel, we don't want to stain this *valuable* silk couch or muss these *expensive* Orientals, now do we?" Dad grinned, cupping her head and drawing it toward his boxers.

Wow! Was I really going to see this? Mom, with her genteel upbringing, had taught us this was a definite no-no. I swallowed hard, my vagina oozing, as Lara worked Dad's enormous cock up through the slit in his boxers, the silken material holding it steady even when she let go. My eyes bulged. Jesus, it was big!

"I like to have my hands free while I work, lover." Her eyes smiled, just staring into his as she teased him, slowly licking the seam of her lips round and round. Then Lara gradually lowered her head toward a dick that was throbbing, the veins pulsing.

My head was down on the little counter, peeking through the slitted opening as her full lips parted, sliding over the spongy head of my father's penis. I barely breathed; I barely blinked.

What's it like to suck a cock? I wondered, my heart pounding with excitement as I tried to move my mouth in unison with Lara's. Dad groaned and when I looked his face was turned upward, flushed and ecstatic.

Someday I'll make a man look like that, I determined, jealous of Lara's power over my father.

Suddenly I flinched, realizing I was kneading my breast, even caressing myself.

I like what I see, I thought in amazement. *I like it a lot*. Two fingers slipped under the edge of my panties, unerringly sliding toward their wet destination as I bit back a groan.

"Turn around," Dad sighed as Lara went on doing things

with her mouth. Things I could only marvel at and try my best to memorize.

Half-dressed. They were half-dressed. I thought it didn't count unless you were naked. I was learning a lot and I was learning it fast.

He caught her by one black-stockinged ankle and whirled her until he caught the naked one, then splayed her over his mouth—and she never missed a beat. How long had they been lovers?

My last view, before I climaxed, was of his tongue burying itself inside her. It took every last bit of energy not to betray myself while waves of release went on and on.

Just as I raised my head my father orgasmed with a shout. A few minutes later he carried Lara to the fireplace and stood her on an old quilt.

"Stand there while I start the fire," he smiled, so different from how he was with Mom. "I didn't get a chance to finish you off."

So there she stood in pulled-down bra, pink garter belt and thong panties. With one black stocking and a single stiletto high heel. I know it's weird, but I felt as if *I* was Lara standing there vulnerable and aroused.

My father, all hairy black chest, now only wore the 'not-neat' boxers that Mother hated. They held hands for a brief moment, and more love passed between them in that instant than I'd seen between my mother and father in a whole lifetime.

I suddenly felt uneasy, is if I'd been disloyal to my mother. Mom would think this woman was a slut. Shouldn't I think the same thing? After all, she was stealing my father away from his wife—wasn't she?

Dad was on his knees behind Lara, and I'd been thinking for so long that the fire was roaring by now. My father certainly didn't *look* like a man being stolen away. Instead he looked...like a man coming home. I bit my lip, my heart contracting as I watched that tender expression on Dad's face.

Aim that look at Mother! my mind shouted. But it wasn't going to be, was it?

Without my noticing, he'd removed her bra, garter belt, and that single stiletto heel until Lara's pink thong and lone black stocking were all that remained of the clothing she once wore.

He pushed at the small of her back and she instantly bent at the waist, her large rounded bottom waving in his face enticingly.

You have to know each other to understand a signal like that, I brooded as I watched him grasp the tiny pink straps of her panties and slowly peel them off.

Why can't you and Mom know each other? I wondered, studying Dad seriously for the first time.

But then Lara stepped from her bit of a garment, so happy and comfortable, and I realized that some things just can't be changed.

"Spread your legs and stay bent," he ordered with mock gruffness.

Lara did as he said, winking back at my father. Dad grinned, calling her an insolent wench, and she threw him a kiss, her eyes filled with love.

Beginning slowly, Dad rubbed his face all over her legs as she stood glowing and all-too-human in that one sagging black stocking. Then, starting at her ankles, he gradually tongued his way up to her knees, going back and forth between her legs, teasing each in turn.

The scene was so erotic that before I knew it my fingers were inside me again. I was breathless at what I was seeing, at what my own father was doing right before my eyes. My panties were soaked and my clitoris was throbbing, begging to climax.

With maddening slowness, Dad licked his way up to and

around her buttocks while Lara and I panted in unison. The scene was hypnotic. I couldn't stop looking and I couldn't stop touching myself.

Do this with Mom, my mind wailed as I slowly climbed toward release.

"Mel," Lara moaned, her eyes pleading.

He was under her at once, doing things with his tongue I'd only seen in a dirty movie my friend 'liberated' from her brother. How weird to see your father do X-rated things to a woman you were trying hard to hate.

We orgasmed as one, Lara and I, she whimpering with delight and I sucking the sound deep within me. It's funny, but I was never able to hate Lara after that.

Gathering myself together, I stood quietly, closing the little serving window even as my father 'finished the job'—as my mother would say. For a moment my eye roamed aimlessly and then it landed on the delicate silk chair, its cover stained with my come. I began to cry quietly–very quietly, because no one must know, no one must ever guess I'd been here.

I looked hopelessly at the chair. *How in hell am I going to clean this thing?*

Weeping softly, I coaxed myself into the far corner of the room. There I sat, huddled among my mother's precious Mettlachs and Waterfords and Royal Doultons, just looking at them while I silently sobbed my heart out.

Things. We certainly do have a lot of things. A wail of pain rose up in me and I bit down hard on my finger so it wouldn't be heard. My eyes fixated on the stained Chippendale chair. I stared and stared at the puddle of come. That one chair came to symbolize the whole problem between my mother and father. An inexplicable rage arose in me.

"To hell with the chair!" I hissed aloud--not very loud, just loud enough to convince myself that I'd finally figured out what was going on.

I gathered my jacket and books and joined my sister at Judy's house. She eyed me curiously. I knew what she'd done. I knew what she'd sent me to see. But none of that mattered. What mattered was our family's future. A future that was obvious—at least to me.

Suddenly my sister seemed years younger than she had earlier. My tears were dry now, my wits collected.

"Everything will be fine," I told her. You'll see I'm right," I consoled a sister who had much to learn. "Really, you'll see. Everything will be just fine."

Saturday
Marcy Sheiner

Saturday morning, ten o'clock, circa 1959: Bobby, Lou and
Frankie come around in a beat-up '55 Chevy Impala, honking
loudly outside my suburban split-level house. I yell good-bye
to my parents, who think I'm going out to do something like
share malteds with the other kids at the corner drugstore, and
fly out the door with my oversized handbag and coat of many
pockets. I squeeze into the front seat between Bobby and
Lou. Frankie waits in the backseat for Judy, who's the last
scheduled pickup. The two of them spend the twenty-minute
drive making out, arousing deep envy in me: I am in love with
Frankie, and in a year or so will act on it.

The guys are all wearing their black and gold Road Rebel
jackets and black derby hats. Cigarettes hang from their
mouths, except for Frankie, whose mouth is busy doing other
things. Every once in awhile Lou's hand wanders over to my
thigh, or Bobby leans over and blows in my ear, which he
knows gets me hotter than a firecracker. I love it all; at fourteen I am thrilled to be one of the cool kids, riding in this cool
car with sixteen-year-olds, flying high on a gorgeous spring

Saturday, adrenaline pumping with anticipation of the hunt and kill.

We are on the way to the local shopping center, precursor to the supersized consumer temples of today. Our stomping grounds consist of about thirty stores. By today's standards the lack of security in these places is astonishing.

We hit the men's store first: we gotta pay our dues up front. We know the guys' shirt sizes by heart: today they've requested purple. Within minutes Judy and I have each stuffed a shirt inside our bags and another one is under my coat. We hightail it out to the parking lot and jump in the car; Bobby makes a big show of gunning the engine and squealing the tires for a dramatic getaway. We take the shirts out of hiding and, as they rip off price tags and change into their spiffy new duds, the boys carry on loudly about how they're going to marry us and rely on their wives for life's essentials. There's some bantering about who will marry me: Bobby or Lou? Maybe we'll live in a threesome. Maybe we'll find and train another girl. Maybe they'll take turns with me. I'm flushed with pride and excitement, despite the fact that the boy I want to marry has his arms wrapped around my best friend.

In those days almost all teenagers shoplifted—a candy bar here, a record album there. But I was no mere petty shoplifter: my criminal activities were on the scale of grand larceny.

During the week we stole every day, primarily candy bars and cartons of cigarettes, the latter shelved right out in the open alongside boxes of cereal and cans of vegetables. On the way home from school we'd pop into the supermarket, stuff the goodies beneath our coats or into our pocketbooks, and walk out without so much as a backward glance.

Saturdays were reserved for our major heists.

Over the years I had several different shoplifting partners, but Judy was the only one whose courage and skill matched mine. We had our own MO: our first stop was Martin's, an upscale department store. We did not covet their matronly clothing, but their shopping bags, a pile of which were on a handy dispenser right near the front door. We helped ourselves to several, stuffed them with books or scarves as decoys, and headed to Lerner's, a midsize, women's clothing chain that is, inexplicably, still in business today.

We took so much from Lerner's it was like our own private couturier. Our routine was to take piles of clothing into the most remote dressing room, try them on with a great deal of noise and giggling, and leave the store with half the items— bathing suits or fancy bras—underneath our regular clothing, or stuffed into our respectable Martin's bags. Occasionally we bought a pair of panties or socks—but the saleswomen seemed to expect teenagers to try on clothes and leave without purchasing anything: these elderly women actually *liked* us. We were always polite and chatty with them, and they'd greet us pleasantly, ask how we were, and even point us to new stock. Why they left us alone in the dressing room I'll never understand. Sometimes we brazenly went back to the bathroom at Martin's to dispose of price tags; sometimes we went to Woolworth's, ate the blue plate special and left without paying. We told our mothers that we traded clothing with one another, and they blithely accepted our lies.

We gained a hot reputation around school. Everyone knew about Judy and Marcy, professional shoplifters. I really needed that stature—I was the only Jewish girl in our crowd, and, even worse, I'd skipped two grades and made it to high school at only twelve. I was pitifully immature compared to my classmates—I *had* to be wild in order to be accepted. Besides respect, shoplifting got me dates and a fabulous wardrobe.

I was caught three times: once stealing records with my sister —but that was at the very start of my career, and it didn't much scare me. The second time I was nabbed boosting a carton of cigarettes and the store let me go with a warning. The third time was serious, and it ended my career—but that was after four years and some ten thousand dollars' worth of goods.

After our raid on the shopping center, we head over to the McNulty brothers' house. Joe and Eddie McNulty's parents are seldom home, and they have a finished playroom in the basement, complete with pool tables. Gina and a couple of other girls are already there when we arrive with our bags of goodies. Judy and I present the diminutive Gina with an adorable size five dress (the smallest size available back in the day) we took just for her. After delivering a half-hearted speech about ethics, she tries it on and drops the superior act. The guys tell imaginative, exaggerated stories about Judy and me, how we almost got caught, or how we'd staggered out of the stores with half the goods in view. We drink beer (also stolen), and turn on the record player. The guys pick up cue sticks and set up the pool balls. In the basement are two beds, one couch, and one armchair—the guys are playing for the choicest make-out locations.

We girls watch absently from the sidelines, doing each other's hair or nails, whispering about the guys. When the game is over, the Platters go on the turntable, the lights dim, and we pair off. The only sacred couples are Joe and Gina; Frankie and Judy. I go off with either Bobby or Lou or Eddie, a decision that is reached by consensus among the girls.

Normally I'd prefer to be with Eddie—he's got an adorable face with soulful blue eyes—but because of the excitement generated earlier, I want to be with one of the guys who's been with us on the shopping spree. So I choose Bobby, who's managed to win one of the beds. It's actually a foldout sofa bed, old and lumpy—but we don't care about busted springs poking out here and there. For teenagers, any bed in a house devoid of adults is luxury.

Everyone settles in for some serious exploration. I don't think anyone else has "gone all the way"—I certainly haven't (I'm saving my cherry for Frankie). The boys try, of course: I climb into this old bed fully cognizant that Bobby will try to get as far as he can with me, and that I'll fend him off as much as possible.

This isn't always easy: making out really gets me hot. I go into some kind of altered state, a way of being that I've found nowhere else. Touching, fondling, kissing—the insecurities and terrors of my awkward adolescence vanish. I'm just flesh and bone, melting into some boy. Bobby is no longer the clown of the Road Rebels, always proving himself by doing idiotic stunts in school or in the candy store. In bed, in a darkened room, with the Platters crooning romantically and heat oozing from every corner of the room, Bobby too becomes a pool of molten flesh, and I can hardly tell where I leave off and he begins. I've discovered ecstasy, and I can't get enough of it—despite the denials of lust that I frequently express, as every good girl must.

Bobby wraps one arm around my waist and the other around my neck and pulls me close. His lips make a beeline for mine, and more or less hit the target. I adjust my head so our lips come together flawlessly, and he sticks his tongue in my mouth. Tongues are a big deal with us—we wiggle them, make circles around each other's, push them in and out, suck on them. I'm an avid tongue-sucker: too avid, in fact—some of the boys have joked that they've suffered from my strong suction skills.

Bobby's trembling hand cups my breast through the fabric of my blouse and bra. We've gone this far before; it's acceptable. He's even taken my bra off and fondled my naked skin. The boys have schooled themselves in bra removal, and Bobby accomplishes it with no assistance from me. I'm already breathless, lying in wait for the delicious sensation of his thumb circling my nipple. Once he does that, and blows in my ear, I'm gone. He knows this, all the boys know how I get from ear play: once, in the car, Frankie and Bobby held my arms down while each worked on an ear. After they'd tortured me to the point where I was humping air, they drove me home and unceremoniously threw me out of the car. This story gets told for years to come.

Tonight, though, Bobby's ear-blowing is focused and sensual—he's not going to abandon me this time. Our bodies come together, and we start to dry-hump. I frequently come from dry-humping, grinding myself up against the hard lumps in the boys' pants. I have never actually seen one of these lumps in the flesh; I only know that it serves my purposes quite nicely.

Tonight I'm aroused far more than usual. I've been feverish ever since I got into the car this morning. My body's response to the shoplifting escapade has been dramatic, with adrenaline pumping from fear and anticipation. All day I've wanted to be in one of these guys' arms. I feel an intense intimacy with Bobby from sharing our adventure. so I'm more willing to let Bobby do with me what he will.

We get sweaty. We grind, grunt and groan. Time stops. I could keep doing this for hours—and we do.

Suddenly I realize that Bobby's hand has left my breast and is snaking down, beneath the waistband of my skintight elastic stretch pants. His fingers are crawling underneath my panties, heading toward my genitals. This is new; I'm not sure what to do, but I know that, at each stage of making out, I am expected to protest. So I reach down and tug on Bobby's hand, slightly pulling myself away. He obediently takes his hand out of my pants and continues with the ear and mouth stuff.

Secretly I want Bobby to try again—I'm curious about

where he's going with this new move. Gina has told me about being finger-fucked: is that what he intended to do? I wriggle around, panting encouragingly, and soon Bobby tries again. This time I let his hand get as far as my pussy before issuing a feeble protest: I pull back, but I leave his hand where it is, and ask in a whisper what he's doing.

"I just wanna touch it," he says, his voice so full of pleading I almost feel sorry for him. I lie passively staring at him while he opens his hand and gently cups my pubic area. His eyes roll back in his head. He moans.

Jesus, what power I possess! Merely touching a part of my body has transformed this goofy boy into a trembling, almost worshipful man. Why this is so I'm not sure, but I feel magnanimous. His fingers tickle my slit. I lean forward and bury my face in his neck so he won't see how hot I'm getting.

It feels like forever from the moment Bobby finds my cunt until the moment he enters it, but it's probably only a minute or two. He parts my lips and slips a finger inside. I pull away, but he follows, staying on target. I'm confused: I want to let him play around inside, but I'm not sure if that would constitute losing my virginity. I worry that he won't respect me, or that he'll tell the other guys and they'll think I'm a slut. I wish I could walk across the room and confer with Gina or Judy—but they're lost in their own hot games.

Eventually Bobby makes it all the way in, and begins pumping his finger in and out, going progressively harder and deeper. The first time his finger hits my cervix I inhale sharply, involuntarily. I don't know what's happening, that this is my cervix; I only know it feels incredible— shocking and thrilling all at once. My mind has turned off; I just want to revel in sensation.

I'm stunned that Bobby's fingers can make me feel this way. I feel like crying and laughing all at once.

In gratitude for the pleasure Bobby's giving me I kiss his

face, his eyes, his ears. I rub his chest, sliding my hand under his open-throated shirt. He grabs my hand and puts it on his bulging crotch. This I've done before: I rub and press the lump. Bobby's fingers slow down.

I don't want his fingers to stop, so I pull my hand away. Bobby groans in dismay and thrusts my hand back into position. At this point I feel that I have no choice in the matter, so I rub and squeeze until he stiffens and utters a little "oh." The hard lump gets mushy. His fingers stop moving entirely. I'm disappointed—but I wouldn't dream of showing it.

Bobby gets up and goes to the bathroom to clean up, and I am left to lie there alone listening to the syrupy sexy sounds of the Platters, marveling at what I've just experienced. When he returns, we cuddle and whisper and laugh about our great shoplifting escapade. *We never refer to our sex or talk about how it felt.*

We hear the others winding down, too, and boys coming and going from the bathroom. Soon we'll all pile into the car and Bobby will drive everyone home. I'll write in my diary. I'll call Gina the next day to tell her about my first finger-fucking.

I'll endure another week of school. Eventually, inevitably, Saturday will roll around again. It's what I live for.

Too Bad

Cara Bruce

I enjoy my own company.
I am my own best friend.
I am unique and special.

Mira looks in the mirror as the words of the subliminal message float over her. She hates the first part of this CD, the part that says the stupid phrases out loud, grinding deep into her consciousness the fact that she is alone. She feels like part of a "Saturday Night Live" skit, but this one isn't funny.

She is trying to get her life back together, to get over her obsession with boys—specifically, bad boys. She hasn't been the best girl her whole life, but the boys she has fallen for have been far worse. They're the types of boys who started smoking when they were thirteen, lost their virginity at fourteen, shoplifted, drank too much, drove without licenses. These were boys she would see huddled on street corners, tongues flickering over bad teeth, hands balled into fists and shoved deep into pockets big enough for stealing. These were the boys she loved.

In a fit of rage Mira grabs a bar of soap and flings it at the CD player. It hits and slides down, not even causing a skip in the CD. A siren sounds underneath her bedroom window. She lets out a half-yell and looks for something to punch.

Mira resides in a small studio apartment, the only thing she can afford in the city these days. Since her resolve to give up bad boys she has barely left it, feeling trapped and timeless, like a junkie—just without the momentary euphoria.

She stares out her window onto the busy street below, where the boys are gathered like ants at a picnic, or roaches, scattering whenever a cop car crawls by, a single megaphone ordering them to disperse.

Mira's first boyfriend was named Tad. He had crazy black eyes, glittering with insanity. He was energetic, bustling, busy—overflowing with a contagious energy that made Mira proud. He dealt drugs, supplying people with ingested happiness and need. He bought her a car and occasionally gave her flowers—acts that Mira now sees as a way to shut her up. A few romantic gestures in a lifetime of cruelty, and they had fooled her. She had thought she loved Tad, and he had tried to keep her. He put her down, took from her, let her take care of him so she felt needed. This was a pattern that hours with her therapist helped her to recognize. She needed to feel needed. Needed to feel loved, important, cared for. And bad boys were the ones who let her do that. Bad boys always seemed to have secrets; she never knew what they were going to do next. It was the uncertainty that got her blood racing—which is why she needed to be needed by them. If she wasn't needed, she would be too uncertain, which made her crazy with lust. Either way, the titillation happened.

Sex with Tad was violent, unyielding. He liked to hurt her—but in those days she was against being hurt on principle. Maybe if she had given in to that one thing they could have reached an agreement and worked everything else out. But Tad was big and strong and Mira's refusal only made things worse. He knew Mira didn't love him. She knew she didn't love him. The only reason they stayed together was his badass reputation. Once he started getting his shit together and stopped doing drugs she grew edgy, anxious, bored. When he calmed down and was ready to admit he needed her...she left amid a flurry of violence and crazy outbreaks, scared, guilty and confused.

Not understanding herself and overly concerned about how other people saw her, she moved on to the next boy, a singer in a punk band whose ego clouded any chance for her to shine. He didn't last long, but still did damage.

After a while she noticed she was staying with him only because he'd been the ultimate bad boy. Her lust for him was built on a faded reputation—and his bad boy behavior wasn't linked to fun things like breaking into churches and baptizing each other; or driving down to Baja, sleeping in rest stops—these were some of the best moments of her life. No, his bad boy behavior was all about *him*—fucking around behind her back, lying, occasionally snorting cocaine. Though he never stopped being a bad boy he wasn't spontaneous, fun or needy enough for Mira. But before she could leave, he did. She didn't care.

By this time she should have been dating bad *men*. There is a difference between men and boys, and these were perpetual boys.

The next one was an ex-junkie—or so he assured her, until her roommate found a syringe under the bathroom sink. In her need and effort to help him she was pulled down with him, swirling deeper and deeper into a place with no air. She would fantasize about his death, exciting herself into a frenzy, becoming convinced that she would come home and find him stiff, a needle poking out of his arm. She drove herself crazy with this ultimate fantasy of not knowing, while he drove himself further into addiction. She was the perfect enabler—yelling at him to do something while he hid in the bathroom for hours trying to find a vein. Yet she couldn't let him go—or maybe it was the comfort of the addiction that she craved. Either way, it took almost losing their lives for them to reluctantly let each other go. Not knowing where he was made her want him again, and she still clung to him emotionally. They talked on the phone late at night, both of them scared of the future and afraid to be alone, each one picking up the pieces of their lives: two steps forward, one step back.

Mira's parents joke that they would be happy with a son-in-law who graduated high school, has never been in jail, and doesn't do drugs. Mira has yet to accomplish that. Almost a year of therapy has only helped reinforce what she's known all along: she has a fetish for bad boys. It's gotten so bad that she doesn't even know where to meet good boys—much less men—anymore. The methadone clinic surely isn't the place. Neither are her AA meetings or codependency support groups. She has no idea where good boys go or what they do.

She avoids people or they avoid her: the circle of money owed is too big to comprehend. She dresses and walks out of her apartment, turning off the CD with its stupid New Age music playing over the sounds of oceans and mountain streams. The only thing the CD is good for is helping her piss. It sure as hell isn't going to help her find a good man. Not that she thinks she needs one; in fact, there are times, more often than not, when she wonders what she will do if she does find a good one. He'll probably stifle her, bore her to tears. She'll become demanding and out of control. They'll end up hating each other. It seems like she can't fall in love unless it's a completely codependent nightmare. Mira's fear drives her into a heated, sexual frenzy; she wants to be done with that.

A craving comes over her as she walks down Mission Street, the music from the CD stuck in her head. Her body is anxious, aching. The familiar feeling of being uncomfortable in her own skin overpowers her. She needs *something*. She thinks it might be drugs, until she finds herself staring at a boy leaning on a pole at the bus stop. He has a faded black eye, a torn leather jacket, and an unfiltered cigarette hanging out of his mouth. She reaches up absentmindedly to rub her shoulder, straining her neck to get a little stretch. She can remember a time not too long ago when she was addicted to exercise, when she had to work out at least once a day so she wouldn't go insane. Now she is stuck on something easier—a quick fix: a Valium, or a fuck with a stranger. She makes a mental note to call the psychiatrist and ask to be put on antidepressants. She has never tried them, but she can't seem to pull herself out of this black hole; besides, those mental magic pills might help with addiction. Or so she has heard.

Mira has a good job, is smart and attractive—yet she stands on line every morning with the dregs of society to drink methadone from a paper cup. If it weren't for the last boyfriend, she wouldn't be here in the first place, though he has taken no responsibility for that. The aging punk rockers in the clinic are like ghosts, flickering patterns of light against the concrete walls of the city. This is what happens to young drug addicts, to all of the bad boys; they simply disappear. Once loved and cared for, they become a burden to those around them, or are simply forgotten as they fade into the background of daily life. But for Mira they represent all the familiar feelings she identifies as want, need, craving—in short, sex.

Still, the realization that her last boyfriend could end up pushing a shopping cart has frightened Mira enough to try to rid herself of her bad boy obsession. She cannot conceive of herself as the type of woman who'd end up with an ex who lives in a cardboard box. She comes from the suburbs and still speaks to her parents once a week. She practices yoga, goes to work, cleans her bathroom. She isn't the type to throw her life away—though she has come close many times now, each time on account of a bad boy.

She goes to the park and sits on a bench, watching the different groups of boys: the Mexicans with their hair slicked back and shirts buttoned up to their necks; the black gangstas with big, baggy jeans and starter jackets; the punk rockers with rainbow hair, black leather jackets and worn jeans. Each group united in the economy of the drug trade. They have their own private financial system. Trade, barter and petty robberies feature brightly. Mira notices a few girls in each group, their loud mouths slashed with bright pink lipstick, too-big jackets that claim them as belonging to one, if not all, of the boys. The girls who hang out with these boys have to be tough, have to hold their own. They are the brassiest, most brazen girls anywhere—but they're also the saddest inside. Some have made the mistake of having children, and walk the line between addiction and mild discomfort, just wanting to be loved. Mira is familiar with those girls.

Mira watches the complex play unfolding before her. Each group of boys is similar in their treatment of the girls. Each group occasionally picks on the girl, until she defends herself with insults, before they go back to ignoring her. It reminds Mira of high school.

A boy comes over and plops down next to her. Mira feels her heart beat faster and her stomach churn. He smells like sweat and cigarettes. He is good-looking, in that rough, unkempt way that she likes. He wears a faded T-shirt bearing the name of an obscure punk band; the scars on his arms tell the tale of where he's been. She bites her lip, promising herself she isn't going to give in to this one. She's stayed off drugs for a few months now; she can stay off bad boys as well.

But fetish isn't the same as addiction: one can be broken, she knows, but she's not so sure about the other.

"Got a cigarette?" the boy asks, looking at her from the corner of his eye. His lack of acknowledgment makes her cunt wet.

Mira huffs in response, yet begins digging around in her purse. She pulls out a battered pack, hands one to the boy and keeps one for herself. The boy pulls out a shiny Zippo and lights her cigarette first. Mira sucks deeply, afraid to say thank you, afraid to look.

She thinks of a poem given to her by a friend, a poem about ex-boyfriends. She thinks how this boy looks like everyone she has ever known. She remembers how lonely she is. She fights the urge to offer him something she has at home, a drink, a bong hit, anything to get him alone. She crosses her legs, tightly. His aura makes her hot.

"What're you doing?" he asks.

"Nothing. I don't know," she says brusquely, wanting to stop the conversation before it gets the best of her. Fighting herself with each breath. "Nothing."

"Well, 'Nothing', what's your name?" the boy chides.

"Mira," she says slowly, deciding whether or not to lie but then deciding that it is too small a city, that she will run into this bad boy again, at a club, a bar, on the street. She always does. Once you meet them it's like they follow you, tagging along like a bad afterthought.

"Figures," he laughs. "Do you know your name means 'bitter' in Hebrew?"

She is taken aback. She considers herself a nice person. More than that, she's blown away that he knows this. A smart bad boy. She almost swoons, imagining him shoplifting books for her, breaking into museums to take her on private tours. She inhales deeply on her cigarette, a blush running up her cheeks. "It means 'marvelous' in Latin," she tells him, enraptured in their private game, this instant intimacy with a bad boy.

"Marvelously bitter," he says, laughing harder. She is turned on by his sense of humor, his ability to smile. She recalls reading that laughter is the best aphrodisiac: it sets off your dopamine neurotransmitters and really does make you feel good. Before this she had thought her dopamine was shot.

The boy is still amused with himself, and this amuses her.

"Are you Jewish?" she asks.

"No," he says, "I just like names."

They are silent for a moment until the boy says, "My name is Max. It means 'greatest' in Latin."

"We both do well in Latin," she says, trying to be funny. The pulsing in her clit tells her that she has given in already.

The boy cracks a smile and asks if she would like to take a walk. They get up off the bench, their simple movement attracting attention from all three groups of boys. He calls her 'Nothing' as they walk; she is touched by the fact that he already has a pet name for her, no matter how degrading.

By the time darkness falls they're at her studio. She presses her answering machine button and realizes that her ex-boyfriend hasn't called yet today. She doesn't care; it's not him, the ex, or the one here now that matter—it's what they represent.

Max has his arms around her in an instant. He is kissing her neck, his snake tongue rummaging in her ear, his hands everywhere at once. She wants to ask him to slow down but doesn't; instead she gives in to it, to the way she feels with a bad boy.

They fall onto the unmade bed and she wishes she had cleaned up earlier. He pulls off his T-shirt and Mira lightly traces the tattoos adorning his chest, trying to imagine how proud they must have once been. He's been in jail, been addicted to drugs, and he never finished high school. He is everything her parents don't want, and everything she does. Mira gives in to his caresses, his unspoken promises. She can already imagine him sitting on her bed, watching TV night after night as she works her boring job, coming home simply because he needs her.

He pulls her closer, as if sensing she's pulling away, and whispers how beautiful she is. She hears his words as shallow; she hears the lies hanging off his voice. But it is exactly this that fuels her, the uncertainty of truth. She kisses him. The room heats up and she takes off her shirt. His fingers deftly unhook her bra, like one who has done this many times before, and he leans forward to suck on her tits until she moans. He runs his tongue lightly over each nipple. His hand undoes the button of her jeans. She reaches down to help him, to speed up the process. Together they wiggle her free of pants and panties. She is naked on the bed and he is still wearing jeans, socks, and boots.

Their kissing is intense and she lets herself go deeper into it. His fingers move down to her pussy and rub her clit. This always makes her happy. Bad boys always know what to do. She moans and raises her hips in encouragement. He moves faster, harder. She bucks and grinds beneath him. Two fingers are now moving at lightning speed over her clit; she breathes harder, whispers *don't stop, keep going, I'm almost there*, and she is, almost there, teetering on the edge. He moves one hand into her, her pussy wet and dripping, his fingers moving upward, outward, as if he really knows where her G-spot is. Two fingers on his other hand continue to dance rapidly on her clit and that's all she needs. She digs her nails into him and swallows his hand with her orgasm. Her thighs tighten around his hips, her head falls back and her cry fills the room.

He quickly pulls out a condom, ripping the tinfoil package with his teeth. She likes the fact that he has condoms on him; he probably fucks a lot. He pulls down his jeans until they rest around his knees. His cock is hard and thick. She's glad he can get it up, she knows too many bad boys who can't anymore, and there's a fine line between bad and useless. He slides the condom over his dick and quickly pushes it inside her.

He moves against her, pushing in deeper, harder. She clings to him, pulling him closer with both hands. He fills her up, his face scrunched in a mixture of concentration and ecstasy. She closes her eyes and lets herself go, hoping for one more orgasm. He thrusts in and out, groaning with each movement, *you...feel...so...good....* She blushes, moans, her hands reach behind for the bedposts. He notices and moves one hand to hold her wrist, tight, the way she likes it, and she likes how he knows this. He pushes deeper as she yells, her cunt again spasming. He gives one final, massive thrust and seems to hang right above her, his feet turning, eyes squished shut, as one tiny bead of sweat drips, landing smack between her breasts.

He falls over on her; his legs still trapped in his jeans. She lies there, staring over his shoulder at the water stain on the ceiling. She counts to ten, as his body grows heavy, wondering if he has suddenly fallen asleep.

"Hey," she whispers, nudging him with her elbow. "Hey, get up!"

Max doesn't move. Mira is trapped beneath him. She groans, *get...up...* as she pushes him to the side and slides out from under him. He remains facedown on the bed, his white, pimpled ass shining.

She shakes him harder but he doesn't move. "Fuck. Get the fuck up. Quit freaking me out," she cries. She grabs her bathrobe off the back of the chair and swats him hard across the ass. For a split second she wishes he had spanked her, like a bad girl.

She pinches his earlobes, a tip she has read in an OD pamphlet at the free clinic. She pulls his head up by his hair. His face is turning blue.

"Fuck!" she screams, suddenly afraid. This fucking bad boy, this good-for-nothing asshole, this stranger, has died in her apartment. She doesn't even know his last name. She crosses the room in hurried steps and dials 911.

"This guy, this guy, he's in my house, he's dead," she pants; she is panicking, afraid. Did she kill him? What will they do to her? Will she be in trouble?

"Is he dead or dying?" the operator asks.

"I think he's dead," Mira said. "I think so but I'm not sure."

The operator tries to calm her down. Mira rattles off her address and the few details she knows. She is wondering whether she should pull up his pants when the operator on the other end tells her not to touch anything.

She gets off the phone to wait for the paramedics. She wonders if they will send the OD combo—the short fire truck and the ambulance. The operator asked her if he was on drugs. Mira said she didn't know; that she didn't really know him at all.

Mira gets up and tiptoes over to him, half expecting him to jump up laughing. She thinks of how pissed she'll be if he does, but she expects him to be an asshole. She pushes him again; he still doesn't move. His body is getting cold, way different than it was just moments before. She thinks this is like a bad urban legend, she is now one of those women that kill men with sex. She wonders if this is a crime.

Mira rifles through his pockets. She pulls out a dirty syringe, a packet of cottons and a cooker, the complete package from the Needle Exchange. She also pulls out a wrinkled ten-dollar bill. She thinks about pocketing it. In his other pocket is a list of phone numbers, scrawled in bad boy handwriting; most of the numbers belong to girls. She wonders if her number would have made it onto the list. She also pulls out his ID card. It's not even a driver's license, just a California ID. His name is

Maximus Pastorelli. It sounds familiar. With some quick math she figures that he is, no, he was, thirty-eight. Even dead he looks much younger. She sits on the side of the bed and pets his dirty hair. She is shocked that he was able to have sex. This makes her think he hasn't used yet, or hasn't been using that much. She wonders if she should tell the EMT this. She wipes her fingerprints off the drug paraphernalia and puts it and the ten bucks back in one pocket, the ID in the other. Before replacing the list of phone numbers she copies them down and hides the piece of paper. Then it hits her. Maximus Pastorelli. He used to play in one of her ex-boyfriend's favorite bands. She even met him once at a party. He was rumored to be clean. For a brief instant she wonders if this event will make her ex-once-removed jealous.

The paramedics come, ask her questions, write down her information, look at the syringe and take him away.

"So did he OD?" she asks.

The EMT points out track marks on his neck. "It could have been an aneurysm," he says and shrugs. He gives her a number to call for the autopsy report.

"You don't use drugs, do you?" the paramedic asks, looking right into her eyes like a high school principal.

She slowly shakes her head no.

"You're a pretty girl," his partner pleads, "You don't need guys like him."

She nods. She finally understands. Bad boys aren't the source of her uncertainty. The real uncertainty is death, which is, also, the ultimate certainty, the final frontier, the last hurrah, all that crap.

She unearths the phone numbers she has hidden and calls one of the girls, hanging up after listening to her say, "Hello? Hello? Fuck you." The girl's voice is raspy, as if she has been smoking since she was twelve. Mira plays the CD of Max's band. She feels as if a huge burden has been lifted off her. His music doesn't even sound good anymore. But she still sits and listens to the entire CD, as if it's a eulogy. She wonders if she should tell anyone what has happened. She calls her ex, the fan of Max, but hangs up when his new girlfriend answers. She showers, dresses nicely, then calls an old coworker, one who dates nice guys, and asks her what she's doing tonight. In mere minutes she has a plan. She applies makeup and brushes her hair. It's like the last time she shot dope—she knew she was done, it was out of her system, she no longer needed it.

Her coworker picks her up and tells her she's changed since Mira last saw her: She no longer dates computer programmers and accountants. Now she dates girls. She takes Mira to a trashy dyke bar. Mira walks in and looks around. The air is electric; it smells like showered sex. Mira has never been with a woman before, and the thought of the unknown makes her pulse gallop.

She spots a heavily-pierced woman smoking under the bright red NO SMOKING sign. Mira makes eye contact, and smiles.

Mail-Order Bride
Saira Ramasastry

My name is Hubert W. Humphrey. Hube Boob. Hube Tube.
Humpty Hubert. Hubris. I've been called every name on every
possible occasion and it's all very funny.

I'm not what you'd call a ladies' man. Though I am
tempted to blame this on my name, it really has nothing to
do with that. My name actually suits me well. I'm big-boned-
-obese, my doctor calls it. I'm short. I don't exercise. My
favorite things to eat are donuts and fast foods. I'm just a
regular guy.

But I have never been able to get a date. My lowest point
was when I asked Harriet, the checkout clerk, to go with me
to the office Christmas party. Harriet is a member of the fat
pack, a group of mall chicks who hang out together during
coffee breaks. She has the least presentable face in the fat
pack—oily skin, pockmarks, and buckteeth to boot. But she
has enormous breasts. I figured if we were in the back of a car,
in the darkness of night, I could bury my head in her tits and
get laid. So I asked Harriet to go with me.

"No way," she responded, "am I going to be a Hairy

Hump!" She walked away, taking her heavenly 40DDD tits with her.

Let's face it: If I couldn't get a fuck out of Harriet, there wasn't much hope for me. I didn't go to college, where women get naked just for the intellectual experience. I couldn't afford a decent whore on my paycheck as manager of the local Kmart—a prestigious job where I come from, but the salary caps at fifteen bucks an hour. Maybe I could find myself a cheap hooker--but with the threat of AIDS and other diseases, I didn't want to risk it.

So I turned to the Internet. Free porn, free live streaming video, free tits—whatever I wanted, whenever I wanted it. No dates, no hassles, no fear of disease. I discovered a site that would change my life: www.XoticMailOrderBrides.com.

It was 3:00 A.M. I had just finished jerking off to some soft porn, but was still unsatisfied. I went to the mail-order brides site and began browsing.

Online, I was the pickiest son of a bitch in the world. I passed over pretty Thai women because I decided they were too scrawny. I clicked past the Russian ones for being fake blondes. Most of these women were stunningly beautiful: a guy like me had no business overlooking them.

I spent hours that night trying to find The One. The One what? The one ultimate fuck of my life is how I thought of it. I like curvy women with thick black hair and easy bedroom eyes. My random clicking patterns weren't bringing her to me, so I consulted the advanced search engine.

South Asian brides came up. Indian chicks? Why not?

I followed the link and there she was: Siliidi. I clicked to see her profile and instantly got hard.

She was practically naked. Her stats were listed on the sidebar: 5'9", 38D-26-38. Her skin was the color of coffee ice cream and looked every bit as tasty. She had great tits—

definitely real—with round, suckable brown nipples. Her hips flared out from her tiny waist and flat stomach. Her legs were long and lean, but had that fleshy female roundness that I love.

With a package like that, I wouldn't have cared if she had Harriet's face. But of course she didn't: she was absolutely gorgeous. Her hip-length black hair was spread across a white pillow, and her huge, liquid brown eyes stared at me as if she wanted to devour me. As if she wanted to fuck me.

I connected to the site and sent Siliidi a private message.

<HUBACCA> Hello Siliidi.

<SILIIDI> Hello there. Who are you? ;)

<HUBACCA> My name is William. I saw your page and wanted to say hello.

<SILIIDI> Well hello, William. You obviously already know my name....

<HUBACCA> Are you in India?

<SILIIDI> No....

<HUBACCA> Where are you?

<SILIIDI> I'm from Sri Lanka. It's very hot here tonight, so I'm not wearing any clothes.

<HUBACCA> Do you look like your picture?

<SILIIDI> Yes, except for one thing.

<HUBACCA> What's that?

<SILIIDI> I'm wet. I want you, William.

She was getting right down to business. I didn't have to do a thing. She proceeded to send a series of dirty messages while I jerked off again and again. Before I knew it, the sun was rising and I had to get ready for work.

Over the next two weeks we continued our virtual meetings nightly. Eventually I sent her a naked picture of myself and told her my real name was Hubert. I didn't want to be caught in a lie if I got to meet her in person. To my surprise, she said my photo turned her on. That night I typed out the things I wanted to do to her while she touched herself. Then I sent her a hot 69 and was completely spent.

Later that night, I wrote her a short email asking if she wanted to marry me.

She was still online. Yes, she said, she would marry me and yes, she would fuck me.

I waited outside International Arrivals for Sri Lankan Airlines Flight 24824. I had given up fast food for a few weeks, so my stomach wasn't rolling over my belt quite as much as usual. I had also bought a new pair of pants; this was as good as I was going to look.

I couldn't wait to meet Siliidi. It wasn't only that I wanted to get regular sex--I certainly did--but this was the first time in my life that a woman had learned almost everything about me and still wanted me. I felt incredible. She was the hottest thing I'd ever seen—at least, there weren't any women I'd jerked off to who were better than Siliidi.

We didn't love each other, but neither of us minded. We were adults, and each of us would be getting something we needed. She wanted a green card; I wanted to get fucked and have my house cleaned. Besides, I genuinely liked Siliidi—and to be honest, I'd never really liked a woman before.

I'd agreed to our getting married in the airport chapel. She had said that if I didn't marry her right then and there, she would get on the next plane back to Sri Lanka. Those were her terms; if it meant getting sex right after I took her home, I was more than willing to oblige.

I saw Siliidi on the security camera as she walked out of customs and shivered—in person she was even better looking than her Internet photo. She wore a sundress tight across her tits. Her hair hung sexily down her back. Gorgeous.

Siliidi pushed her luggage cart towards me, showing off, swaying her hips. I shoved a bouquet of airport flowers in her face and waited for her to speak. I was sweating profusely. I couldn't wait to finally hear her voice. She turned out to have the voice of a phone sex operator. I got hard instantly.

"Hubert, have you been dieting? You are *so* handsome," she intoned in her lilting Sri Lankan accent. She took the flowers and inhaled them as if she wanted to eat them. Even that got me hot.

All I managed to say was a charming, "Hello, Siliidi. You look very nice."

She grabbed me by the collar and kissed me as if she had been missing me intensely. She wrapped her luscious arms around me and squeezed. "Marry me now, Hubert," she whispered.

She had traveled halfway around the world to be with me, and I wanted to be with her more than anything. We parked the luggage cart at the chapel, went inside, and tied the knot.

Strangely, Siliidi didn't say a word on the way home from the airport--she just massaged my cock. If I had just come to a new country to marry some stranger, I think I would have felt something, had lots to say, questions to ask. Not Siliidi. She smiled calmly and stared out the window, crossing and uncrossing her legs. She asked a few questions about the town. I pointed out the supermarket, local bar, dry cleaners and coffee hangouts. She nodded and smiled, and touched me some more.

We arrived home. Siliidi was impressed by my suburban house, and I guess it did seem pretty big compared to the trailers down the street. It has white vinyl siding that I clean on a semiannual basis, and a moderately mowed lawn. As far as the interior, I was hoping that Siliidi would redecorate and make it nicer.

I carried Siliidi's suitcases inside and let her look around for a while. I could hear her slow, sexy footsteps clicking through the rooms. She made it from the bathroom to the bedroom, and then there was silence.

"Siliidi?" I called. No answer. I walked towards the bedroom.

"Siliidi? Where are you?" I was too nervous to have a hard-on. I crept into the bedroom.

She was standing naked on the bed in a pair of high heels, admiring herself in the mirror. She looked like someone straight out of a live streaming video. My cock banged against my boxers. I'm sure I was drooling out of the corner of my mouth. There on my bed with the *Star Wars* comforter and matching pillows was the sexiest woman alive—who also just happened to be my wife.

The spiked heels caught me off guard. "Where...in Sri Lanka...did you get...*those?*"

Siliidi jumped off the bed and slapped me across the face. "You dirty boy," she said, unfastening my belt and unzipping my fly. "Pull those down. Now."

Though I can get hot about being dominated once in awhile, this was not the way I had planned our first fuck. But I decided to pull down my pants, because it would bring me closer to actually getting laid.

She circled me, but didn't touch me. My eyes lowered to her nipples; they looked like the chocolate icing on mocha cupcakes. I wanted to press my lips to her smooth skin and suck, but I was interrupted by a painful blow across my buttocks.

"Take off your shirt and your boxers," she growled. "Get completely naked."

"Ouch, you bitch!" I whimpered, rubbing my butt. I wanted to tell her to fuck off, but if I upset her I might miss the fuck of my life.

I stood naked in the middle of the room. Though I had shed a few pounds across my midsection, I was still fat and pasty white. My man breasts wobbled over three rolls of stomach flesh. My cock, though above average in size by most standards, was dwarfed by my fat. I was sure Siliidi would make fun of me.

But she didn't. She got down on her knees and her face turned soft and gentle. She touched my cock as if it was a precious thing to protect and cherish. She took it in her mouth and worked it between her luscious red lips, moaning softly, like a woman eating her favorite dessert.

I grabbed a cluster of her raven tendrils and moved her head up and down my cock. She sucked harder; moaned louder; applied more pressure to the tip. My ass tightened and I felt an orgasm starting. She stopped abruptly.

She dragged her nails up my chest and looked at me with narrowed eyes. "You have displeased me. Now lie down!"

"What?" I covered my red raging cock with both hands and took a few steps back. "What kind of crazy bitch are you?" What had happened? Things had been going so well.

Siliidi pushed me down on the bed with a surprisingly strong movement of her arms. She raised her leg over me, enough to give me a shot of her wet lips, and kneed me in my doughboy stomach.

When I saw that she was dripping, I calmed down a little. Maybe this was part of her game. I reminded myself that I had an actual, real live female in my bedroom who was wet and ready.

"Apologize to me," Siliidi said.

"For...?"

Siliidi grabbed my belt and whipped the pillow next to me. "Just do it. Do it or never get fucked." She straddled me so her wet cunt was near the tip of my cock. She softened again, turning from bitch to loving wife, and stroked her wetness to remind me she wanted it.

I was so weak—and so close to satisfaction. When I felt her juices on the head of my cock and saw her fondling her breasts, her confusing games didn't matter. I meekly told her I was sorry, though I did not know for what.

She took three minutes to sit down on my cock, making me beg every thirty seconds to go further inside her. I had never seen such developed thigh muscles on a woman. She was able to freeze her toned body just to torture me. Finally, I figured out what she really wanted.

"Mistress," I said, "I will be a good boy. Please, please sit down on me."

I had guessed correctly: she loved my obedience. Now she turned sweet and tumbled down onto my cock. Pressing her hands on my chest, she worked her body over me vigorously, providing maximum pleasure. She brought my head close to her breasts so I could fondle and suck while she moved up and down on me. Using every muscle in her strong and sculpted legs, she pushed me in and out of her.

I had intended to keep it going for a long time, but since this was my first real fuck, it lasted only five minutes—still a record over my hand jobs.

Siliidi looked no more than twenty, so I was stunned to learn that she was actually thirty-five. She had been married once before, to a man with a turban, but she divorced him once she realized he had no intentions of moving her to New York City. Ironically, after they were divorced her ex-husband had wed, in an arranged marriage, a much younger American-born Indian. After that Siliidi became even more determined to get to the United States.

Her parents couldn't arrange another marriage for her, since divorce branded her "damaged goods." So she took matters into her own hands and put herself on the exotic mail-order brides site. She told me she had gotten over a hundred hits a night.

Most of her clients were Germans with brown-girl

fetishes. She didn't get much American traffic through her page; American men seemed to want the petite East Asian types. I had been the first American man over eighteen to enter her site.

Was she as desperate as I was? Apparently.

When I realized this, I really fell in love with Siliidi.

In our home, Siliidi ruled. Outside, though, she played the role of the subservient woman, turning me into a living legend in our small town. For instance, every Wednesday she would come to the Kmart with a basket of homemade curries and breads as if she were delivering my lunch. I hated Sri Lankan cooking, but these lunches served an important purpose: every man in Kmart noticed her. She wore a tight spandex miniskirt with no panties, and the curves of her ass showed through the shiny black material. Her tank top, in some loud color like turquoise or yellow, revealed plenty of cleavage, not to mention the outline of her nipples. The men at Kmart couldn't believe that I had married this exotic beauty with "a tight ass and a nice rack"--and that I had her wrapped around my little finger.

"Hubert!" she would call, running through the store, sending her breasts flying up to her chin.

"Hello, Siliidi," I'd repy in an aloof manner. To the guys around me, it looked like I had everything under control. She wanted me; I could care less about her. (Inside my pants, of course, my erection was almost ready to pop.)

Siliidi embraced and kissed me; I just stood still. "I made you some special treats because I was thinking about you, Hubert!"

Her voice was syrupy sweet. I wanted to melt, but I remained cool--and all the staff could see it. I pointed to my office with the plastic furniture, and blinds on the windows. "In there," I told my wife.

Siliidi bowed with a sexy flick of her waist. She ran her

hands hungrily over my blue polyester uniform and tugged at my name tag. She left the food on the customer service counter and we went into my office. I closed the blinds and moaned loudly for a good five to ten minutes while she gave me head—which anyone in the vicinity could not help but hear. I would munch on a cafeteria hot dog I'd bought earlier so I wouldn't have to eat Silidi's curry. I loved eating lunch while having my cock sucked. Later I'd throw the Sri Lankan food out in the dumpster, carefully wrapping it so nobody would see that I hadn't eaten it.

This thing that I had going with Siliidi couldn't last, and I knew it. She was eventually going to get her citizenship, and then she wouldn't need me anymore.

After two years in the United States, she was losing her accent. Now, when she told me to strip, she could have been any woman in a porn video. She was losing her uniqueness. I still got instantly hard at the sight of her, but I was less than satisfied with our sex. At first Siliidi had been so exciting, I had to have her, I needed so badly to be inside her. Now, while we were fucking I would think about the stale Twinkies on top of the refrigerator.

One night Siliidi was sitting on her side of the bed smoking a cigarette. She extinguished it only halfway through. "I get my citizenship next week," she said.

Siliidi wasn't desperate anymore. She moved out a few months after she got her papers from the government. I didn't try to stop her.

Sexually, Siliidi had spoiled me. I hadn't jerked off for the entire two years we were married, and I didn't want to jerk off again. Sex with a hot kinky woman with humongous tits had turned out to be everything I'd always wanted, at least in the beginning. Now, I want it again.

But I am faced with the dilemma of being Hubert W. Humphrey—a middle-aged, obese, pasty white, fast-food junkie with a middle management job at Kmart. I may not be the most pathetic man in the world, but I'm never going to be an ace on the singles scene. And I still can't afford a classy whore.

On the Internet, though, I'm a king. I choose who to get off with and when. On the Internet, there are women who need me--women even more desperate than I am.

So, I'm back to XoticMailOrderBrides.com. I've even lowered my standards. Now, I chat with them all—scrawny Thais, fake blondes from Russia. After all, you never know when you might find a woman who's desperate for a green card.

Kamini's Story
Cheyenne Blue

She was Kath's friend, as I remember, and was staying with Kath for a week. I think she normally lived in Chicago-
-somewhere cold and damp and gloomy, anyway. Kath brought her along to my place for our girls' night.

"This is Kamini," she said, and I nodded hello to the small, bird-like person with glittering dark eyes. She was wrapped in a huge scarlet sweater and olive-green leggings and she wore a lot of gold jewelry; thick ropes of it covered both her wrists and I glimpsed more under the wide neck of her sweater.

I poured them each a glass of wine and we chatted as we waited for the others to arrive. They came together; Nerida entered first, shedding scarves, beret, jacket, and purse as she always did, dropping them in brightly-colored puddles in my small hallway. As usual, she was talking fifteen to the dozen as she accepted the glass of wine I gave her, waving it around in emphasis of whatever small point she was making. She drained her glass, while I took Monica's coat and placed it more decorously over the back of the couch.

I refilled everyone's glass along with Monica's. Nerida was drinking fast and when she does that, which she doesn't do often, our nights always travel a different path. I smiled at the thought--such uninhibited nights were fun. I hoped Kamini was up to it.

By ten o'clock we had the world's problems solved, our husbands and boyfriends reduced to smoldering rubble, our children in mental asylums; we were giggly and in a hazy state of mild intoxication. Nerida passed around a joint and we each inhaled and coughed with illicit daring.

I noticed that Kamini drank less than the rest of us, although she chortled and joined in our banter, trading insults with Monica as if they had shared the same cradle. She was older than the rest of us, I surmised, maybe in her midforties, though her caramel skin showed few signs of aging; it was darkly smooth, silky in the way that only clean living can maintain.

Nerida inhaled the last of the dope, coughed and leaned forward. Through streaming eyes, she said, "Let's play two rounds of Draw Jacks."

I groaned; I still remembered the last time we'd played this game, derived from Nerida's imagination. I had lost the first draw, and had to recount my brief office affair, the one I hoped Phil never found out about, in explicit and embarrassing detail.

Nerida's game was simple. We posed a question, and then everyone had to draw from a deck of cards in turn. The first person to draw a jack lost, and had to answer the question in as much detail as the others required and with total honesty. Of course, in all our history of playing, there never had been a non-sexual question.

Kath was explaining it to Kamini, who nodded. Yes, she'd play.

"The question is," Nerida leaned forward with shining

eyes, "How did you lose your virginity? Details. Who with, where, what, how, positions, feelings...everything. I almost hope I lose the draw; I've got a great story to tell," she said, smiling wickedly.

We all thought her idea a good one, so without the spirited debate that normally accompanies the question decision, we agreed. Monica shuffled and fanned the deck out on the floor. She drew the ace of hearts.

"Omen," she laughed. "Maybe I'll get lucky when I go home."

Seeing as she'd just been describing her husband's performance problems and how she'd been reduced to sneaking crushed herbal potency enhancers into his food, this seemed unlikely. We rolled around the floor laughing again.

The deck must have been down to nearly half when Kamini drew the first jack. The others scooted back and propped themselves against the couch, settling in for a good listen. I poured more wine and curled up on the floor cushions in the corner.

Kamini seemed unsure of how to begin; she looked to Kath for reassurance.

"Just spill it," encouraged Kath. She turned to the rest of us. "I haven't heard this story either," she said.

"All right." Kamini settled herself on the floor cushion opposite me and crossed her legs Buddha style.

"I grew up in India," she began. "My family was very traditional, and though my sisters and I were encouraged to be independent, there were always some things that couldn't be changed. As Hindus we were vegetarian, we dressed modestly, and we were expected to follow professional careers as befitted our station in life. We were also expected to marry young and to marry the person our parents chose for us."

"An arranged marriage?" I asked.

"Yes." Kamini looked at me and smiled slightly at the

expression on my face. "I know, it is hard for you to accept, but it never occurred to me to question it. I truly believed that my parents knew best."

Nerida arched an eyebrow. "Really?"

"Yes. I was young and naïve, even by our standards." She paused and took a mouthful of wine before continuing. "The man my parents picked out for me was one of their friends. He was a good, honest man, a doctor in our community. His first wife had died five years before, and my parents wanted to please him, as well as ensure my security. He was sixty-four years old."

"Your parents married you off to an old man?" Kath was agog.

"Yes."

"And on your wedding night, what was he like?" Monica cut to the heart of the matter.

"I lost my virginity the week before my wedding night." Kamini was smiling slightly. "Remember, I was young. I was distraught over my parents' choice for me. I had known they would choose my husband, but in my imaginings it was always someone young, dark-eyed and dashing. Not a kindly, benevolent old man, wrinkled with the passing of the years, with a paunch and drooping eyes. I was horrified. I pleaded with my mother to reconsider, but she refused to listen." Her mouth crooked up at one corner. "Family honor was at stake." She took a sip of wine. "My mother was a lucky woman. She had married a man whom she had genuinely grown to love. And I can only imagine that they had a happy and fulfilling sex life, because if she hadn't, I doubt she would have done what she did for me."

Nerida leaned forward. "Which was?"

Kamini smiled a slow, secretive smile. "I've never told this to anyone," she mused. "My mother knows, of course, but no one else. Can I have some more wine?" She held out her glass, which I rushed to fill. If the wine lubricated her tongue then she could have my entire cellar; anything to keep this intriguing story moving along.

"Three days before the wedding, my mother came to me in the night. She woke me up, then placed a finger over my lips. 'Silence,' she said. 'Don't say a word.' I was accustomed to obeying, so I sat up in bed, curious, but obedient. 'Come with me,' said my mother.

"I was surprised when she led me out of the door and across the fields. The moon was high in the sky, and the glow painted the furrows with an eerie light."

"Did you have any idea where she was taking you?" Kath's eyes were huge in her pale face.

"None." Kamini flashed her a white-toothed grin. "But it was not my place to question. She led me to a house on the outskirts of the village. I knew whose it was, but I had never been there. My mother called once, softly, and a figure slipped out of the shadows. 'I have brought her,' my mother said. 'My daughter. Treat her well and gently.' She took my hand and placed it in the hand of the stranger. I felt calluses, and dry, rough skin, a lizard paw. Then she left, walking back down the path we had taken.

"I called after her, but there was no reply and she quickly faded into the shadows, her sari floating like a ghost. I wondered if I'd dreamed her, and if I was really there at all, but then a hyena yipped, and a breeze carried the scents of a warm Indian night over me, and I knew that it was real. I was scared. I was with one of the oldest men in the village; older even than my intended husband. I didn't know why my mother had brought me here; secrecy and illicit deeds were written in her actions. I tried to pull my hand away, but the old man held firm. He didn't say anything, just led me toward his house. I started to struggle. Everyone knew who lived there with him--his simple son, a brawny boy, maybe a few years older than I was. He didn't leave the house much, but sometimes he could be seen feeding the chickens or shuffling around the yard. It was said that the old man took his son out on moonlit nights to work the fields; some said he pulled the plough like an ox. No one had ever dared to go and find out, but the old man's fields were tended, and no one was ever seen working them in the daytime." Kamini stopped here, and drained her glass.

I looked around the room, to see how the others were taking this story. Kath was staring at her friend, a puzzled expression on her face, as if she was reconciling the Kamini she already knew with this exotic stranger who told such a compelling tale. Monica was leaning back, her eyes half closed, dreamily absorbing the narrative. She would be the one to ask the probing questions later. Nerida was leaning forward, her chin propped on her hands. No one, it seemed, wanted to break the cadence of Kamini's story.

"He led me into his house and pointed to a chair in the corner. 'Sit down there, girl,' he said. His voice was gruff, as if he used it infrequently, but his tone was kind. Not knowing what else to do, I sat. He went over to a counter and started mixing together ingredients with a pestle and mortar. Dried herbs, a pinch of this, a puff of that. When he was satisfied, he tipped the bowl into a pottery vessel and filled it with water. I was afraid he was going to make me drink the concoction, but he passed me, pushing aside the sacking that separated the main room from the sleeping area. He left the divider open and I could see his son. He was restrained on the bed, lying so still that I thought he must be asleep. Or dead. He was naked except for his undergarments. His skin gleamed in the dim light. I don't know what made me do so, but I crept up closer to see. The son's eyes opened. They were wild, not afraid, as if he was fighting something in his head. The man released one of his arms, and handed him the drink he had prepared. The son's hand shook as he drained it, deep, in one go.

"It was strange what happened next. The old man waited a minute or two, sitting on the edge of the bed, stroking his son's hair. Then the son spoke in Gudjarati –my language-- but his accent was peculiar. The words were liquid, falling gently into the room. Gudjarati is a harsh, staccato tongue, full of short syllables, but the young man's tones were soft and flowing--so much so that I forgot to listen to what he was saying, I was so caught up in the rise and fall of his voice. The old man moved around the bed freeing his son, who sat up and placed a gentle hand on his father's face. There was no animosity in his voice or gesture, not what you would expect from a prisoner greeting his jailer. It was more like a benediction.

"Then the father spoke. 'I have brought you another young one,' he said. 'Kamini is her name. Her mother has paid for you to treat her kindly.' The son's eyes shifted over his father's shoulder and found my face. As I watched, his eyes grew calmer. I felt like I was watching someone shift and settle into his own skin, feeling his way into his body. The old man took my hand and placed it in his son's, then turned and left.

"The sacking between the rooms fell into place, a harsh rustle of sound. Some moonlight filtered in through the open window, a tide of light fractured by the shadows of the night. I had a moment of disorientation from the strange room, the eerie events that had led me to this point, an unfamiliar hand in mine. I swallowed once, and the sound was loud in my ears. I wanted to look around, to try and bring some sort of normalcy to the situation, but I found I couldn't look away from the young man. I wondered what his name was, if indeed he had one.

"'Dinesh.' He spoke so softly, the name seemed simply to

materialize in my mind. I stared at him, wondering if I had imagined the syllables. 'Dinesh,' he said again. 'My name. You wanted to know.' He stepped forward on silent feet, and raised a hand to my cheek. 'Trust me,' he said. 'This is for you.' Leaning forward he placed his lips on mine. A soft press, a gentle brush, the scent of cumin and bay leaf, the sweet mother's-milk taste of his breath.

"I wondered where the wildness of insanity had vanished to, but it vanished from my head even as I thought the question. Dinesh's hands were moving with deliberate sweeps over my body, from my cheeks, down over my neck and shoulders, feathering down my arms with delicate strokes. I shivered under his touch, as fluttering fingers of heat uncoiled within me. I wanted him to touch me in new places, forbidden places, the places I'd heard about, whispers from the older women in dark corners. Giggles behind fingers. And as I thought these shameful thoughts, his fingers found the neck of my sleeping garment, and edged underneath to my shoulder. His head was silhouetted against the moonlight, and he moved forward again, so close I could feel his breath, and he set his mouth on mine."

The story had us all entranced--as did the weaver of the tale. The lighting was low in my small living room, and Kamini was sitting on the outer edge of the light. She was still cross-legged, her hands resting palms up, fingers lightly curled on her thighs--a meditative posture. But her head was thrown back; her eyes were closed, the lashes dark crescents of shadow on the gold of her skin. Her throat and long neck were exposed, arched as if for the mouth of a lover. I found I wanted to press my lips to her neck, taste her, absorb her story through her skin. When she swallowed, the ripple of her throat mesmerized me. I wanted the taste of exotica, the fragrance of spice, cardamom-rich, and the added dimension of hearing the susurration of her voice telling the rest of her story.

I did nothing of course. I sat with the rest of my friends, letting her softly spoken words wash over me, redolent with the irresistibility of a first seduction.

"It was the first time I had been kissed," Kamini continued, "and the thought of the touching of tongues was faintly disgusting, the sort of thing I whispered about with my friends. But when Dinesh parted my lips with his, and gently slid his tongue into my mouth, it was anything but. A light probe became a wet, entangling exploration. It wasn't an instinctive thing for me, though. I forgot to breathe, and had to break the kiss to gulp air in loud, panting gasps. He didn't seem to mind, though; he just moved his mouth to my neck, sliding up to my ear, then back to that spot between my neck and shoulder."

I ran my own hand up my neck, imagining the warm glide of lips. My gaze was still on Kamini, envisioning her long-ago encounter.

"His hand slid underneath my shift, then skated further down to tickle the side of my breast. I wore nothing underneath, so when his fingers moved further over they brushed my nipple. The sensation was so new, so wonderful. The fingers moved away, but crept down my side, bunching my loose shift as they moved. The rough cotton dragged over my thighs, sending new sensations over me. My mother's reason for leaving me here was now clear; she wanted this for me, so I didn't resist. He held the hemline of my shift in his hand, then released me and pulled it over my head, so that I was naked in front of him.

"I was embarrassed. I couldn't remember ever having been naked in front of anyone before, certainly not a stranger. My sisters and I were encouraged to be modest, not to flaunt ourselves. 'A quiet dignity', my mother used to say we had. So I blushed, and lowered my eyes from his face, uncomfortable. He was standing so close that when my eyes dropped

I saw the swelling under his ragged undergarments, barely contained. I wanted to touch it, see what it felt like, see if it felt as hard as it looked or if it was spongy, an illusion. I had seen my father naked once, saw the shriveled thing between his legs--but it wasn't like this. My fingers reached out, but I hesitated. I wasn't sure if what I wanted was the right thing. 'You may,' Dinesh said, and took my hand and placed it on himself. My fingers touched the hard swelling, and I jerked back as if I'd been scalded. It was so hot, and there it was like a paradox, the butter-soft skin, silky over steel hardness."

Someone in the room sighed softly, an exhalation of longing. Kamini had described it so perfectly. The unbelievable hard softness of a man there. And that first moment of discovery.

"He took my hand and led me to the bed. I felt that magical moment of inevitability, as I knew what would happen. I welcomed it, accepted it. And my acceptance made me bold, and I lay down on the bed, and drew him down with me. Our bodies moved together. I felt my nipples brush against his chest. I felt his thigh slide over mine. His body was golden, like a warm carving come to life. My hands explored; his did too. He did not let me get too bold, but stilled my fumbling caresses as he pushed me back and lowered his mouth to my breast. Ah, that first suck, the pulling on my nipple, that tug—it was like there was a cord running from my nipples to parts of me I couldn't even name. Each time his teeth slid over my nipple they pulled the invisible cord that seemed to connect my nipples to my sex.

"And his hands stroked down my body, so lightly I felt as if he brushed each tiny hair, each goose bump, into awareness. His hands moved with such incredible slowness; an aimless wandering, or so it seemed, but there was a purpose, because where his hands moved, his mouth followed. He said words against my skin. I don't know what they were, or why he said them, but his mouth was moving and the words were absorbed into me so they were never spoken into the air. His breath against my skin and his words, though I couldn't hear them, were now a part of me and would stay with me always.

"His fingers crept over my belly. When they reached the edge of my pubic hair, he hesitated. His mouth was buried in my stomach. I moved my hips, a small thrust up, to encourage him, although for what I wasn't really sure. His fingers moved down, tangling through my hair, and he slipped a finger into me. I was wet, so there was no resistance. No tension—just a need for something I couldn't put into words. And then his mouth followed. There, at the point where it all comes together, his tongue pushed into me, stiff, and then he lapped me like a kitten, lapping over my clit, and all the wanting and the tension and the wonder knotted together into this implosion of feeling between my legs and I came."

I'd closed my eyes during Kamini's narrative, the better to absorb the essence of her tale. I opened them now; her head had fallen forward, her raven hair hiding her face.

"I'd never had an orgasm before, and it was wonderful. I felt I was drifting somewhere in the stars of the Indian night, out there in the warmth and the earth and the small night-time noises. And maybe I was; who is to say whether any of us truly inhabit our bodies at those moments? And though I was satisfied, I knew we were not done. Because I knew the final movement of this night would be for him to take my virginity, to pierce me, open me up for future loving. I know..." There was self-deprecating humor in her voice. "Such old-fashioned words. Such male words, dominating words rather than sharing ones--but that is how I perceived it then.

"Dinesh was still between my legs, his mouth still whispering incantations against my flesh. His breath was cool against my wetness. He lifted his mouth from me; I felt the loss, but then he moved over me, a night-shadow of a man, looming against the moonlight, and before I could cry out or react in any way, he pushed himself inside my body.

"I knew it was coming and I was poised to cry out in anticipation of the pain my mother had taught me to expect, but my cry was swallowed by his mouth. We lay, locked together, mouths, sex, and for that moment, souls. For all my readiness, for all his consideration, it still stung. Not the tearing, ripping pain I had been told about in vague terms, but a stretching, a fullness, a rawness of flesh. He waited, unmoving, until I flexed my leg around his side, then he started to withdraw. I was so innocent that I believed it was over. I didn't know of the repetition, the tidal rhythm, so I whimpered in protest. Then he slid back in slowly, deeply. And I learned the dance and followed his lead, and we moved together until he stiffened and cried out against my neck.

"I felt the slip of his seed out of me, as he lay on top of me, unmoving. And then he started to shake, a deep trembling that wracked his body, and he raised his head and looked me in the eyes, and they were the eyes of a stranger, not my gentle lover of a moment ago, but confused and wary. Cat's eyes. Tiger's eyes, wild and predatory. I raised a hand to his face, stroked his cheek, and he turned his head and bit me, hard, with sharp pointed teeth. I jerked my hand away; the blood oozed, a bead of crimson. He moved towards me again, lapped the droplet away, then moved off and out of me in one fluid movement. He moved over to the other side of the room. I lay unmoving, my legs still parted around the echo of his body, the sticky trails of his seed over my thighs.

" 'Go,' he said, and the words were harsh, no more liquid words of song against my neck. 'Go now.' And he turned away from me, so that I saw his buttocks lit by the moonlight, and I saw his shaking.

"I was scared again, and in my terror all rationality was

gone. I thought of men-beasts, of soul-crushers, of mythical shape-changers. I grabbed my shift, pulled it over my head and blundered out into the main room. His father was sitting silently on a stool in the corner. Our eyes met, a brief exchange of meaning, and then I ran out of the house, across the fields, through shadows, past the small creatures of the night, over the furrows. I tripped and fell, and lay for minutes with my pulse pounding in my ears, the metallic tang of fear in my mouth, dirt under my fingers.

"When I reached home I realized I could not enter unseen. So I washed in the animals' trough, splashing cold water on my awakened flesh, on my face, between my legs. I wrapped myself back in my shift, and waited beside the shed until morning. My mother was the first person up in the house, before the servants even, and I slipped inside under the cover of her movements and snatches of song. She sang louder than usual this morning."

Kamini fell silent, as if wondering how to finish her story. "It was never spoken of," she said finally. "My mother never mentioned it, and a week later I married Jamal. He was a good man. Kind."

"Did he realize you were not a virgin?" My voice sounded husky to my ears.

Kamini smiled slightly. "No. I was wise enough to know that I must pretend I was untouched. And I think that he interpreted my fear of discovery as fear of the wedding bed, and he treated me gently. He died four years after the wedding, six months after he brought me to America."

I thought of Kamini, young and alone in a foreign country.

"Do you know what Dinesh's illness was?" Monica was analytically curious.

"No. Some form of mental illness I think, but I am not versed in such things." She looked at her hands, tightly clasped in her lap. "And I do not want to know. I want to keep the magic."

"And do you hear from your family in India?" Nerida touched Kamini's arm lightly to get her attention. "Do you hear of Dinesh?"

"My mother and sisters write to me, but they do not speak of him. Why would they? But both of my sisters married a few years after me. I wonder sometimes if it was the same for them."

Envy
Eden Lenz

"Love me?" he asked, as I stepped into the foyer.

Goose bumps rose on my bare arms in the suddenness of the air-conditioning. I gripped the back of his neck, pulled his face to mine, and ran my tongue over his lips in lieu of an answer.

A woman's voice broke our embrace. "Where'd ya run off to, Tom?"

"Who's that?" I mumbled against his mouth.

"That'd be Marissa." He nipped my lower lip. "Best not keep her waiting."

I followed Thomas into the living room. A petite brunette lounged on one of the white couches. I vaguely remembered meeting her once before. What stuck with me was that I had envied her breasts, hidden behind a baby-blue T-shirt. Little perky ones. "Plum titties," as one of my college boyfriends would say.

Thomas introduced us.

"We've met," I said, being very snippy about it. I was already seething at the chance I was taking by having an affair with my husband's partner. *He's wasting my time*, I told myself. *And if this is some ploy to get me to say that I love him, he's wasting his own time as well.*

He seemed to pick up on my mood change. "Help me with the coffee?" He motioned toward the kitchen. "Marissa, why don't you go for a swim?"

"You're not getting rid of me that easily, Tommy-Boy," she said. "And we're not having any coffee. How dare you try to close me out of the afternoon? After all, I came here especially to meet this one you've been raving about." To me she added, "I hear you're into it."

"Into what?"

"Don't be coy," she said, walking toward me, a panther stalking her prey. "He's told me about you. You do it all." Marissa lifted one thin strap of my camisole top from my shoulder and slid it down my arm. "He thought you'd be into a little two-on-one action; he thought you might like me, too." She did the same with the other strap; willpower was all that held up my top.

"Marissa..." Thomas's voice was full of warning.

"He said you'd do anything for him."

Caught in her gaze, I breathed, "Did he?"

Her feline eyes tilted at the corners as she smiled and eased my top down to my waist. "I agree, Tommy. She has beautiful breasts," she purred.

"I sometimes wish they were smaller." Thomas was watching intently; I wondered if he was surprised that I let her touch me. He couldn't have been surprised at her. I felt he'd chosen her on purpose, almost as a test.

"I wish mine were bigger," she said. "Nice and round, like yours." She squeezed my breasts. "Ooh, and obviously real, too." She leaned down and inhaled my nipple, then pressed her tongue against it.

Thomas was pouring scotch into three glasses of ice; I could just see him in my peripheral vision. "A little relaxation?"

I was melting into Marissa, regretting my earlier curtness. Neither of us answered him. I leaned against the mantelpiece behind me and stretched out my arm for support, nearly knocking a Waterford vase from its perch.

"If this is going to happen, ladies, let's move the festivities downstairs."

We regrouped in the finished basement, where a pool table stood in the center of the room. A beautiful bar, leather-padded around the edge, lined one wall. The room was decidedly more masculine than the upstairs décor—the rooms that any visitor could see.

Marissa downed her whiskey right away and slinked off to the pool table. She stripped quickly, except for a garter belt and black stockings. Then she lay down on the pool table and began writhing, her legs bent and her heels digging into the corner pockets. "Come here," she said, wriggling a finger at me.

I took a sip of my scotch and knelt in front of her. She smelled wonderfully clean and feminine, like expensive French soap. I thought she wanted me to go down on her, but that wasn't the plan. I wanted Thomas to watch, to burn with envy. I glided my fingertips over the insides of her thighs as she unsnapped her garters.

Thomas knelt behind me, wrapped his arm around my waist and sucked the curve of my neck. "I want you," he breathed. Something pressed into my belly, harder even than the cock he pushed against my ass.

"I want you," I repeated. "I'll do anything."

"Say you love me."

I sighed his name and tilted my head back against his shoulder.

"You want to show me?"

Nodding, I scraped the insides of Marissa's thighs, leaving pink trails of raised skin in the wake of my fingernails.

His lips never leaving my skin, he said, "I want to watch you get fucked."

My shoulders fell. I wanted *him*, not her. I fell asleep every night with my back against my husband's and my hand between my legs, thinking of Thomas. I didn't know what to say, short of "I love you," so I said nothing.

"Why don't you trade places?" he suggested, pulling away from me and standing up.

I found my voice. "Why?"

He smoothed one hand over my cheek. "I told you why. I want to watch you." Thomas helped me up on the table, onto my knees, facing away from both of them. "Will you let Marissa fuck you for me?" he asked. "You said, 'anything.' Remember?"

"She'll let me," Marissa said, wrapping the silk stockings she had just stripped off around my knees, binding them tight. I kept still and pressed my face into the table. "Hand it over and keep an eye on her."

He put the instrument in her hand: a smooth, slender vibrator that looked to be made of black leather.

"Put your ass high up in the air." Her authority thrilled me and I obeyed, but I consciously did not do my best. "I said high in the air, you little snatch," she scolded, slapping my ass. I did as she asked.

Thomas came into my view; he was perched on a barstool, holding his swollen, purple-tipped cock. I wondered if he was all right. I worried the thrill had melted, like the ice in Marissa's empty glass.

"Now keep your eyes open and do not look anywhere but at his face. Do not watch his cock; that's mine." A warm trickle of oil slid down my crack; she rubbed a thicker substance with the consistency of petroleum jelly onto my asshole.

The oil smelled like citrus, lemon-lime with a hint of orange.

My knees were pressed together but I felt deliciously exposed. She rubbed the dildo against my pussy lips, rolling it in my juices. Without warning she leaned up and placed it against my lips. "Taste yourself," she demanded.

It was sweet with the taste of the oil.

"Are you ready for a fucking? You may only speak by saying yes or no. Is that clear? If you say yes, I continue and if you say no, I'm going to fuck you even harder. You want it like that, right?"

"Yes." My body trembled with anticipation. She plunged the vibrator into me, turning it up full blast right away. It felt delicious; I closed my eyes for one second.

"I told you to keep eye contact with him, slut."

She let go of the humming toy and its full weight pressed against the front wall of my cunt, against my G-spot. With both hands she slapped my asscheeks simultaneously and dug in her short fingernails.

I strained against my silken restraints to part my legs. Thomas flinched and began to stroke his cock, slowly, almost absentmindedly. I ached for him to fill me with it. I began to understand what was happening. *He wants to see me controlled. Can't he do it himself? Doesn't he realize the power he already holds over me?*

Before I could think again, Marissa removed the vibrator and turned it off. My pulse pounded in my ears. "What do you want, little snatch? You want to be fucked? You want to really be fucked? Hard and fast, or slow and deep, baby? You want it?"

"Yes, yes," I moaned.

"Then I get to do what I want to you. With your legs tied up, you don't have much choice do you?"

"No."

"Then I'm going to do what I like. I know this is what you

want," she hissed. Marissa teased my asshole with the thin tip of the vibrator. She wriggled it around a bit and then slid it slowly inside. It was pure pleasure. Marissa knew what she was doing. "You've been ass-fucked before, haven't you, you cunt?"

She began to pull the vibe out, but then plunged it in more deeply instead, twisting it in the same repetitive motion.

"You've had a cock in your ass, haven't you? You liked it. You want it again." She thrust the vibrator into me down to its base. "You want his cock shoved up your ass while I eat your cunt."

Marissa held the vibe still so I responded, "No."

"No?"

Thomas's face was hazy. My eyelids were getting heavy. "No. No," I said, trying to get the pleading, eager tone out of my voice.

My plan worked. She grabbed the end of the tool with both hands and pumped it furiously up and down, sometimes twisting it or rolling it between her palms. I could feel the orgasm building and knew it would be explosive.

The juices and oils collected around my clit and I strained my ass higher in the air. All the while Marissa kept up her monologue. "No? You don't want that big cock up your ass? He'd fill you up till your cunt ached. He'd get you to spread your legs wide, bitch. I'd get underneath you and tease your little clit and suck his balls while he fucked you. If you were very lucky, I might stick my finger up your cunt too. Maybe two fingers. You don't want that?"

"No," I managed to moan. Marissa moaned herself, and while she plunged the vibe in and out of my ass, she started to rock back and forth. Just when I was about to come, she removed the vibrator. Thomas's face came into focus and I realized that he had already come. I was wondering if that meant I was out of an orgasm when I felt Marissa untie the stocking. She was as breathless as I was. I wished Thomas would take over the game and send her somewhere else.

"On your back," she purred. I rolled over; the felt of the pool table was rough against my bare skin, except for where my ass lay on the cool, smooth mahogany edge. "Spread."

I opened my legs, entwining my forearms around my calves, grabbing my ankles and pulling them as close to my ears as I could for her. She twisted the vibe up into my ass, all the way up. "You don't want this, do you?"

"No," I whispered, looking straight into her cat-like eyes. With one quick motion she turned the vibe on and up to its highest setting. Then she placed her tongue flatly against my clit and lapped at it. I tried to keep repeating, "No, no," so she would be rougher, but "Yes, yes" kept coming out of my mouth.

"Yes?" she paused to ask. I could say nothing, only moan as she pressed her thumb against my clit. She let go of the vibe, as she had done before, and I again felt its fullness. "Spread more."

I let go of my ankles and put my elbows against the backs of my knees, pressing them down into the pool table.

"Did you say yes to me you little slit?"

I gathered my senses together enough to think of a way to test her and said, "You'd better fuck me, whore."

Without a word, she got up and walked over to stand behind Thomas at the bar. I mouthed, "I want you" to my lover.

A smile slid across his lips. His eyes grabbed mine and refused to let go.

"Please," I added.

He took another sip of his drink and whispered, "Say you love me."

I turned my head and inhaled the scent of sex in the close, heavy air.

Marissa returned to my side, holding a large double dildo. "Take that thing out of your ass and move back on the table," she said. "I'll teach you to talk to me that way."

I did as she said, once again stopped cold on the verge of orgasm. *Who is she to control my pleasure? His pleasure? Some cruel sexual puppet master? But Thomas is the one who wants this. Obeying her is obeying him. Fucking her is fucking him. Coming for her is coming for him.*

She climbed up on the table and stood above my hips. "Show me that hot cunt again." I obeyed her and resumed my position as she squatted above me, our pussies almost touching. She leaned back, supporting herself with her hands on the mahogany. She was dripping wet.

The dildo slid easily between her hairless lips, slipping deep inside her, up to the middle. The cocks were pink, the balls in the center redder. She twisted and thrust it in and out of her cunt. Then suddenly she knelt over me, as she had before, steadied herself on the table and grabbed the dildo with her free hand. She moved so that we were perpendicular, her heel against my hip and bearing her weight on her other leg.

"Get ready," she growled. She forced the giant dildo straight down into my cunt and started sliding up and down the other end, her tiny breasts thumping with every beat.

We both moaned loudly when she thrust my end all the way inside me. Her pussy smashed into mine and we writhed against each other, our clits touching haphazardly. When they did, I imagined tiny electric sparks shooting from them.

Her muscles were twitching and it was almost more than I could bear. I came hard, bucking and scratching at the felt surface, moaning for my observant lover.

She withdrew the dildo from my cunt and hers. By the time I realized where I was again, her mouth was on my clit. I kept coming: small delicious fluttering orgasms.

I opened my eyes to look at her and saw Thomas, pounding her from behind as she leaned over the pool table eating me. He had one arm wrapped around her slender waist but I couldn't see what his other hand was doing. "Tell me what he's doing to you," I said, grabbing her hair and pulling her mouth from my cunt.

She spoke with intermittent panting and moaning, "He's fucking me...fucking my ass, feels so good...has his fingers up my cunt...just two, ohhh," she moaned, "Oh fuck, he's got three, fuck." She bit her lip and tried to put her head down but I yanked her hair again.

"How many now?" I demanded, mimicking her dominatrix tone.

She said nothing but let out a squealing moan and threw one leg up on the table. She mumbled something.

I said, "I can't hear you, whore, yell it. Shout out what he's doing to you."

Thomas's body was still but his arm moved furiously. She wriggled in his embrace.

"Where is his cock?" I shouted.

She mumbled again, so I repeated myself, adding that she'd better yell.

"My ass," she moaned, saying it over and over until she was finally meeting my demand that she yell. "His cock is in my ass, all the way in my ass."

Thomas had stopped thrusting into her. From the movement of the muscles in his shoulder and arm, I knew he was up to something. "What is he doing to your pussy now?"

She ground her hips into him and said clearly, "He has all his fingers in me. He's...oh...he's sliding his hand up...fuck...up inside me." She squealed a little on the word *inside*.

She bit her lip and kept her eyes closed. I was about to demand that she keep talking, but she went on without my instructions.

"He's made his hand into a fist. He's rolling it around against my cunt. Beautiful," she moaned into her arm, "feels so beautiful."

I saw Thomas's arm move faster; he twisted his wrist with every thrust inside Marissa's wetness.

"He's fucking me with his fist," she said, louder than before, like she wanted to hear it and knew that I didn't. "Harder. Harder, you fucker."

He pumped her for a few more seconds, then slowly withdrew his hand. She opened her eyes and looked hazily at me before saying, "Oh! Oh, oh, oh yes. He's in my ass again. Feels so good. Filling me up. Yes. He's pressing his hand against my clit. He won't let me come yet. I have to come. Let me eat your pussy; let me eat you."

With a quick, cat-like motion, she wrapped her arms around my thighs and pulled my cunt to her mouth. I sat up, spreading for her as much as I could and grabbing the back of her head. Her tongue was furious, plunging deep inside me, lapping at my clit. She sucked and licked me like a starving woman.

"She's going to come," Thomas told me. I laced my fingers around her head and pressed her hard against me. She screamed into my pussy and bucked against his increasing thrusts. As her wails subsided into moans, Thomas's eyes fixed steadfastly on mine.

I loosened my grip on Marissa, who kept licking at me, though with less enthusiasm than before. I hated her for coming. For having the orgasm I had been denied at my lover's hands.

"Tell me you want me," he said, driving his gaze deep inside me. "Tell me you love me."

"Mmm, yes, mmm," she said, coming up for air, wearing an expression of absolute bliss.

Thomas continued to insist, "Tell me you want me, you love me. Say it, say it." He lost himself in his own voice as he closed his eyes, breaking the spell, and came.

"Ooh, yeah," she moaned, as he finally withdrew.

I got off the table and Marissa took my place, curling up like a shrimp and falling into an immediate, sound sleep.

"You didn't say it." He reached for my hair.

"That's right. I didn't."

"You're a strong one." His eyes narrowed with a repressed, amused light. "I'm going to wash up. Be right back."

She was never the one in control, I said to myself as I poured another scotch. *He was. The puppet master. She was his mouthpiece. His eyes held me tighter than any restraints could have. He fucked me through her. Still, I didn't get what I came here for. What I'm risking everything for. His hands. His kisses. His cock. His release. The soothing of my desire.* I pushed myself onto the barstool Thomas had used like a crow's nest. *Maybe I do love him. But I'll never confess it. I'm not ready for that level of control.* Taking a sip of my drink, I stared at Marissa and envied the contented rising and falling of her small breasts.

Plain Women
Lisa Prosimo

As a boy, I was adored. My mother said the highlight of her day was dressing me in my sailor suit, or some other charming outfit, and taking me to the park. "People stopped to stare," she was fond of saying. "You were always so handsome."

I'd catch her gazing at me, beaming, as if I were the grandest prize anyone could ever receive. I know why she was particularly proud to be my mother: she was plain. It was astounding that a woman so unbeautiful, together with a husband whom many considered ugly, could produce a child so fair.

After my father died when I was four--a terrible work-related accident—my mother and I would sometimes lie in bed gathering love, like warmth, from each other. We'd play a game called, "Who's the best, most beautiful boy in the world and who is lucky enough to be his mother?"

In truth, I was the lucky one. My mother was sweet; she had the truest heart of any person I've ever known, and I am privileged to have learned so much from her. She died shortly after I left for college. I miss her to this day.

As a man, I am adored. I am not being immodest when I say that I can have just about any woman I desire. I am handsome, successful, and easy to get on with; therefore, I am sought after. Dazzling women slip me their telephone numbers all the time.

But I do not seek the company of dazzling women. Some of my friends think I'm insane, but really, where's the challenge in being with the perfect body, the exquisite face? No. It is the unadorned woman that presents the challenge. I learned long ago the art of reaching past the austere appearance of a lady to get to the secret person of the heart. Inside each bare root a rose waits to blossom.

And what lovely bouquets I have gathered. Once, while traveling alone through Europe, I met a middle-aged couple and their adult daughter. Being the only Americans in a small Italian *pensione*, we naturally gravitated to each other, often having dinner and taking in the sights together. Constance, the daughter, seemed to shrink in my presence, withdrawing deeply into herself and hardly speaking a word. For days, I couldn't tell the color of her eyes because she refused to look up at me. Her mother confessed that she and her husband had coaxed Constance to take a sabbatical from teaching to visit Europe with them.

"She's never been anywhere," said the mother. " 'How much longer will we be here?' we told the silly girl. 'We're getting on dear, you know. Do travel with us!' "

Constance was so shy she was nearly transparent, yet I sensed in her a resource worth tapping. The hint of a smile, the way she moved her head, revealed the rich emotion that had lain buried under the surface far too long. Why should a woman so sweet remain unfulfilled?

After a long day of cathedrals and museums, I suggested dinner at a bistro in a nearby town. "Oh," said the mother, "my feet are killing me. Father and I thought we'd take supper in our room tonight."

I turned to Constance. "Would you do me the honor of dining with me this evening?" I asked. She immediately brought her hand to her throat and looked away; her face turned a bright pink.

"Oh, go on, dear," said the mother. "No need to worry about us. You go have dinner with Jeffrey."

Constance picked at her dinner, her eyes never leaving the plate. I leaned over and took her hand. "You hardly said a word on the way over. Do I make you uncomfortable?"

She looked up, blushed, and pulled her hand away. "No," she stammered, then, "Yes, you do."

"Why?"

Constance picked up her glass of wine and downed the ruby liquid in one gulp. "Because I don't know what to make of you."

"Why make anything of me? Why shouldn't two people who enjoy each other's company have dinner together?"

"Why do you enjoy my company? I'm not a sterling conversationalist, or…"

"Yes?"

She took a deep breath. "Why me?"

I took her hand again, turned it over and kissed her palm. "Why not you, Constance? You're a lovely woman."

I didn't expect tears, but there they were. She shook her head. "No, I'm not," she said. "You're making fun of me."

"I would never do that," I said.

"I'm not pretty and I have a terrible figure. And I'm boring."

"No, you are not boring." I took a handkerchief from my breast pocket and dabbed at her eyes. "I would very much like to make love to you, Constance," I whispered.

From her expression, it was clear that she was stunned. After a long moment of silence, the questions in her eyes dissolved and she nodded.

"My parents..." she began.

"I'll take care of that," I said.

I secured a room at a hotel and left Constance in the lobby while I phoned her parents and told them, "I'm afraid we've had some engine trouble and won't be able to get the necessary part until tomorrow."

Actually, I believe the mother knew I was lying, but she only said that she understood the problem and wished us a good night's sleep.

I found Constance sitting on the bed with her head in her hands. I sat beside her and gently took her hands from her face. I kissed her.

"What do you want me to do for you?" she asked in a small voice.

I smiled. "No, Constance. What do you want me to do for you?"

"Oh...I don't know."

"Yes, you do. Tell me."

"I want you to...touch me."

I drew her into my arms and slowly pulled down the zipper on her dress, pausing along the way to kiss her back and caress her skin. She moaned. "Does this feel good, Constance?"

"Oh, yes. Yes."

Her skin was soft and smooth. My hands traveled down her torso to her hips and stopped at her panties; then I slipped my fingers under the lacy material. She shivered and I could feel chills rising on her skin. She bent her head forward and I kissed the back of her neck, then peeled the dress from her body. With slow and deliberate movements, I finished undressing Constance.

First I removed her bra, pausing to kiss and lick each breast. Although not heavy of flesh, she had lovely large nipples that responded to my tongue by getting wonderfully hard. I ran my tongue along her legs as I rolled down each stocking. Easily her best feature, her legs were long and shapely and as smooth as satin. I licked between each toe and she moaned some more, lay back, and rested on her elbows. I pulled her legs over the side of the bed and knelt on the floor in front of her. My hands went to the elastic of her panties and she lifted her hips while I pulled them down. I rested the flat of my palm across her mound, moving it slightly, subtly. Her body rose against my hand; she cooed, trying to keep the sound secret; then I moved my hand down lower and parted the lips of her cunt. "Ahhhh," she moaned, a cry simultaneously seductive and revealing.

The bed was one of those wrought-iron things popular in Italy at the time. Someone had hung a necklace over one of the spikes and forgotten it. As Constance moved beneath my hand, the jewelry made a chiming noise that added just the right music for lovemaking. I pulled her cunt lips apart and slipped two fingers deep inside. She churned against my fingers, flooding them with her juices. My thumb whorled over her clitoris and as she continued to writhe, I murmured how wonderful I thought she was, how lovely. I brought my tongue to the tip of her clit and slowly, repeatedly, licked the soft flesh. She pushed against my mouth, as if my tongue were the key to opening her most secret place, as if she were giving herself over to me. I sensed her coming; heard her crying, whimpering; then felt the swift spasms of her orgasm. When her convulsions had subsided, I withdrew my tongue and lay beside her. She turned to face me, tears in her eyes.

"That's never happened for me before," she said softly.

"But it should," I whispered. "And often."

She put her hand on my chest and smiled, and in that moment, she was radiant. "You still have your clothes on."

"Would you like to undress me, Constance?"

Constance nodded and began to pull the clothes from my body. She didn't kiss me or caress me as I had her, but that was fine. I wanted her to do whatever she felt moved to do, to enjoy and discover the wonder within her. When she had finished undressing me, she stood shyly at the foot of the bed looking down at my swollen cock.

"For me?" she said, a hint of surprise in her voice.

"For you," I assured her.

Constance lay next to me and rested her face in the space between my shoulder and my ear. "I've had sex three times in my life," she breathed. "But always in the dark. I've never seen a man up close before. May I look at your...May I look at it up close?"

"Of course you may look at--does the word *cock* unnerve you, Constance?"

"I don't think so. At least, not when you say it."

She brought her head close to my cock and as her eyes traveled up and down, her face took on a glow of happy astonishment. "So many ridges and veins."

I looked down. My cock was standing straight up, shining from the silky fluid that dripped onto my stomach. I moved my palm over the head and spread the drops across the glans. "Would you like to touch me, Constance?"

"Yes," she said, and moved her hand to my cock in a tentative caress. It took only a few moments before her hand seemed sure of itself and began to lightly stroke the shaft up and down.

"Does touching me excite you?"

"Yes. I love that line of soft, dark hair that goes down your belly. And--it--your penis looks meaty and hungry, and I like that, too."

I placed my hand over hers and moved it to my balls. "And these?" How do they feel?"

"Heavy, full."

Her other hand crawled around past my hip and grabbed my ass. I lifted myself up closer to her face. "What do you want me to do with it, Constance?" I said teasingly.

"Put it in my mouth."

"You do it."

Constance's lips came down on my cock slowly--soft, wide-open, and wet. I held her hair away from her face so that I could watch her mouth take me in, deeper, further. I hardly moved at all; it was all her doing, her show. Soon, she was sliding her tongue down the sides and over the head. She even moved her mouth off my hard-on to take my balls and gently suck the taut skin. Now she was driving me toward the edge, this woman who had thought herself ugly, but who now opened to me like the beautiful flower she truly was. I felt my climax building and carefully withdrew from her mouth. I pulled her up and kissed her. My hand rested between her legs and her cunt gushed against my fingers.

"You're so hot and wet. Do you want me to fuck you now?"

"Please. Yes. Now."

I kissed her again as I sank into her. She groaned against my lips and I swallowed the sound. My thick smooth cock rubbed against the walls of her cunt. Her heat was exquisite. I watched her face as I slowly drove in and out of her. She took up my rhythm, her body rising to meet my thrusts. Her eyes were closed and her cheeks flushed, passion transforming sallow skin to cream and honey; the fire in this woman had completely changed her countenance. This was the look I loved to see in a woman; this was the look I worked so hard to evoke.

Constance began to peak, and so did I. Together we moved into that realm where flesh is everything and nothing at the same time, intensity and dissolution striking simultaneously. I watched the moment arrive when her face was allowed--no--

expected to turn grotesque, twisted by lust, knowing that my face reflected the exact same intensity.

A few days later, I moved on to France and Constance and her parents flew home. But it was a new woman who boarded the plane to Wisconsin, one whose eyes and smile were softer, whose skin was more supple to the touch, and whose attitude had been transformed. That day, a true beauty left Italy.

There have been many like Constance. Women thin or massive, noses bumpy, skin coarse. Some have been flat-chested, or heavy-thighed, perhaps carrying certain infirmities. But all, in some way, are beautiful: treasures who come in plain wrappers. Like my wonderful mother, God rest her soul.

Lap Dance Lust
Rachel Kramer Bussel

We pull into the shadowy parking lot in some corner of Los Angeles. I look around the deserted area, wondering where exactly we are, only half caring. Most strip clubs in L.A. are located in tucked away corners like this one.

I'm a little apprehensive as we walk around to the entrance and part the strings of beads to enter Cheetah's--a strip club, a real live strip club! I've been dreaming of just such a place for years, but have never worked up the courage to actually go, until now. I'd heard that Cheetah's was "women friendly," and from the crowd I can immediately tell it's true. There are plenty of guys but also a decent number of female customers who look like they're having a good time.

My three friends and I take ringside seats along the surprisingly empty stage and animatedly set about checking out each new dancer. Many of them are what I expected--peroxide blonde, fake boobs, very L.A. and very boring. Some have a spark of creativity, and feign a glimmer of interest to tease out one of the dollars we hold in our hands, but many pass right by us or stare back with vacant eyes.

We watch as one girl after another maneuvers around the stage, shimmying up and then down the shiny silver pole, twisting and writhing in ways I can't imagine my body doing. It feels surreal, this world of glamour and money and lights and ultra-femininity. I look and stare and whisper to my friends. Though I'm having fun, the place starts to lose its charm when I have to get more change and still no girl has really grabbed my eye. I settle in with a new drink and a fresh stack of bills and hope that I won't be disappointed by the next round of dancers.

When the next girl walks out, I'm transfixed. She's the hottest girl I've ever seen. She's wearing cave girl attire, a leopard print bandeau top and hot pants--all tan skin, natural curves and gleaming black hair. She looks shiny, like she's just put on suntan lotion. She slithers along, making eye contact when she passes us, crawling back across the stage, putting her whole body into the performance. She toys with her shorts, thumbs hooked into the waist, before sliding them down her long legs to reveal black panties. I know that she's the one for me, that I really like her and am not just an indiscriminate ogler, when I realize that I preferred her with her shorts on.

After her performance, I offer her a wad of dollars. "Thanks," she says. "I'm Gabrielle."

"Hi," I say shyly. "I really like your outfit."

"Me too," she giggles, then smiles before waving her fingers and gliding off the stage.

"Ooooh, you like her. You should get a lap dance."

"Yeah, get a lap dance! Get a lap dance!"

My friends are practically jumping up and down in their excitement, making me blush.

"Maybe."

"No, no, you should get one. She's totally hot."

"I know, I know, but let me think about it, okay?" They're

so eager for me to lose my lap dance virginity, I'm afraid they may drag me over to her.

I need to get away for a minute, so I go to the bathroom. To my shock, I find her sitting inside, casually chatting with a friend. "Oh, hi," I stammer. "Is this your dressing room?"

She laughs. "No, but it's almost the same quality." I smile at her and then go into the stall, nervous at having spoken to her. When I emerge and begin to wash my hands, she admires my purse. I tell her about it and then take out my sparkly lip gloss. She asks to try some, and I hold it out to her, watching as her finger dips into the red goo. We talk a bit more about makeup and then she says, casually, "Did you want to get a lap dance?"

Did I? Of course! "Yes, I'd like that," I say.

"Great, just give me a few more minutes and I'll come get you."

I practically float out the door and back to my friends. *I'm going to get a lap dance, and I arranged it all by myself! Ha!* I feel like gloating. I wait patiently, trying not to let my excitement show in a big stupid grin.

After a few minutes, she emerges and summons me, leading me to the other side of the stage, against a wall where I've seen other girls pressed up against mostly old men. She seats me on a plastic-covered couch, then takes a chair and places it a few feet in front of me. "So people can't look up your skirt," she tells me. I smile to thank her for her kindness; it never would've occurred to me. I give her some larger bills, and we talk for a minute or two before a song she likes comes on.

And then, quite suddenly, it starts. She pushes me so my head is tilted back against the wall, the rest of me pressed against the sticky plastic, my legs slightly spread. She stands between my legs, then leans forward, pressing her entire body along the length of mine. She smells like sweat and lotion and some undefinable sweetness, and I breathe deeply. Even her sweat smells good, like baby powder. Her soft hair brushes against my face and shoulders; her breasts are pressed up against mine. Then I feel her thigh against my hand; she's climbed up on the couch with me. This is definitely not what I expected. I've never been to a strip club before, but I thought I knew the deal--I'd seen *Go*, right? You can't touch the dancers or you'll get kicked out. But what if they're touching you? What about her hand gliding along mine, the outside of her smooth thigh touching my arm, her slightly damp skin setting mine on fire? The look she gives me is priceless: as her body moves downwards and she's crouched near my stomach, I look down and her hooded eyes are on me, her face a vision of pure lust, her mouth slightly open. I'm sure it's a practiced look, but it feels as real as any look I've ever received, and it enters and warms me.

I think I know what I'm getting into; I've read all the feminist arguments, the sex worker manifestos. This is just a job and I'm a paying customer: one song, one lap, one transaction. But all of that background disappears, likewise my friends, my family, L.A., everyone else in the club. It's just me and her, never mind the music; it's that look as she slides between my open legs. I swallow heavily. I can't move, and I don't want to, ever again. I just want to sit here and let her brush herself against me again and again as I keep getting wetter. And then her hand reaches up, delicately turning around my necklace, a Jewish star. It's the sweetest gesture, and something only another femme would notice or care about. She gives me a little smile as she does it, and I give her one back.

The song is almost over, and she gives it her all. Her body pushes hard against mine, pressing my chest, stomach, thighs. She's working me so good this huge bouncer walks over and glances at us suspiciously, but she turns around and gives him a look that tells him to move along. I like knowing that whatever she's doing with me is enough out of the norm to warrant the bouncer's attention. I feel ravished in a way that I've never felt before; it's pure sexual desire, concentrated into whatever messages her skin and her eyes can send me in the course of a five-minute song.

When the song ends, I give her a generous tip, and she sits with me for a little while. She takes my hand in hers, which is delicate and soft, and I revel in her touch. It's tender and sensitive, and I need this, need to hear her sweet voice tell me about her career as a singer, her friendship with a famous musician, her upcoming trip to New York. I need to hear whatever it is she wants to tell me, true or not. My head knows certain things; this is a strip club, that was a lap dance, this is her job. But inside, *inside,* I know something else. I know that we just exchanged something special. It wasn't sex or passion or lust per se; it was more than, and less than, each of those things. It was contact, attention and adoration. Call me crazy, but I think it went both ways.

After we talk, I go back to my friends, but I feel a bit odd. I know they were watching, but did they see what *really* happened?

"That was some lap dance."

"Yeah, that was really amazing for your first time."

"She gave you her real name? That's a big stripper no-no."

"I think she liked you."

I nod and respond minimally, still in my own world. For the rest of the trip, whatever I'm doing, wherever I am, part of me is still sitting on that plastic-covered couch, looking down at her, breathing her scent, reveling in her look.

I haven't gone to any more strip clubs since, or gotten any more dances. How could they ever live up to her? I don't know if I want to find out.

The Price She Pays
Michelle Scalise

A revolving silver disco ball painted a thousand stars over their silhouette as they whirled across the dance floor. She was giving him a hard-on, but more important, she wanted *me* to know the effect her movements were having on the guy. She whispered something in his ear, her small hips grinding into him with a blunt promise.

Billy Idol screamed out of the speakers for more, more, more.

A few members of the wedding party danced around the couple. Less than thirty people remained, all reluctant to leave an open bar.

I played with the roses and baby's breath wilting in the centerpiece and waited for Juliet to finish her game. The guy looked like an investment banker. Expensive suit, prematurely balding but with a hint of sexuality in his glance, as if he were growling under his breath. There was nothing subtle about the expression in her eyes. She had an infatuation for that clean, Armani, white-bread type. Just the thought of turning a yuppie boy nasty got her wet. Not that she had the nerve to act on it--she just liked to play with them, make them think she was going to do things to them they'd only seen in the porn movies their wives were sure they didn't own.

Her brother and his new virgin-white bride sat in a corner with a display of empty bottles, feeling each other up, too drunk to remember they had a honeymoon suite waiting for them upstairs.

When the deejay took a break, Juliet returned to our table, out of breath and flushed. The dark red bridesmaid's gown she'd been so careful about earlier in the day now appeared as if it had been balled up in the back of a closet.

"Cathy," she said, adjusting a few stray dark curls that had escaped the Victorian hair clip I'd bought her. "This is an old friend of mine, David Taylor. Our parents have been best friends forever. And somewhere over there is his wife, Maryann."

There was no need to point her out. David's significant other was obviously the pinch-faced blonde glaring daggers at his back from across the room.

Juliet clutched his shoulder as she stumbled a bit. "We haven't seen each other since my high school graduation, right?" She smiled at him in a certain way: I knew what that look meant.

"Cathy," she continued in her innocent baby doll voice, "he doesn't believe you're my girlfriend. Tell him we live together."

"Where's the restroom?" I asked as kindly as I could manage. "Your dress is a little lopsided. I think we should go straighten you out."

Juliet gave a slightly tipsy laugh. "Oops, she's right. What would I do without her?"

I gave David a backwards wave as I dragged her out into the empty hotel lobby.

"Hey, you're hurting me," she cried. "Oh boy, more

booze." She reached out, grabbing the champagne someone had discarded on a table next to a stack of brochures.

I took her down a flight of stairs and swung open the ladies' room door, but the sound of someone getting violently sick stopped me. Glancing around, I spotted the men's room and grinned.

"Come on, Princess," I said, pulling her along like a puppy.

"We can't go in there," she said, struggling in my grasp. "Cathy, are you upset with me? It was just a dance."

I kissed her painted lips. "Bullshit. You knew what you were doing to him." Then I bit down hard enough to make her yelp.

The small outer area of the men's room consisted of a green couch and two small tables. Quickly checking the rest of the bathroom to make sure we were alone, I shoved her into one of the stalls, slamming and locking the door behind us.

"Lift your gown," I demanded, taking the bottle from her hands.

Juliet stared down at the tiled floor, pouting. "Can't you discipline me at home? Please?"

I didn't say a word, just waited, adjusting the white lace of my blouse. Slowly, she raised her dress up past her tiny waist. Her bright green eyes studied the floor behind me for any sign of incoming visitors.

"I'm sorry," she said. "You know I didn't mean anything by it."

I forced her to stand like that, admiring her shaved cunt— she wore no panties--for a full minute before I let my fingers drift across her inner thigh. Juliet sighed and trembled once, whispering, "No, hey..." I let a chuckle loose deep in my throat and drew my nails against the inner folds of her lips, just enough to elicit a moan from her. She was so wet that my hand was immediately sopping. I thrust a finger halfway into her.

"You're dripping," I said, pushing deep enough to feel her heat, her hunger. "Did you get off on grinding into him, slut? I'll bet you fucked him in high school."

The bathroom door creaked open. Juliet tried to lurch away but I pulled her back. I pressed her further against the toilet, taking the lobe of her ear in my teeth, then licking down the length of her neck, where her veins bulged thick as cigarettes. She moaned at my throat.

"Maybe I should let him watch me finger you," I breathed softly. The man was pissing about six pitchers of beer into the urinal. "You think you can get him hard too?"

Juliet shook her head, curls falling in her face. I pushed her to her knees and raised my black velvet skirt. "Do a good job and I might excuse you," I hissed with enough venom to make her wince.

Juliet's tongue was cold and wet against my clit. I held her hair tightly in my fist, driving her head down between my thighs. "Show me what a good whore you are."

I wanted my juice splashed over her face, wanted to see her back in the ballroom with her cheeks shining, the taste of me staining her lips.

The first man left and another entered.

I arched my back, my orgasm building against her sweet mouth. As the first spasm took hold, everything was forgotten but her tongue buried inside me. When I finished I yanked her to her feet. She was smiling.

"Am I forgiven now?" she asked. "You know I just do it for kicks."

I grabbed the champagne, making her sweat out my answer. A voice outside the stall called: "Juliet? Is that you? Are you all right?"

"Oh shit!" she whispered, grabbing my arm. "It's David. Please don't say anything."

I suddenly realized it might be fun to call her dare, to play out her game to the end for once. Wrapping my arm around her waist, I pushed her out of the stall. "It's both of us, David." Juliet tried to turn back, but I wouldn't allow it.

Instead I forced the bottle to her lips. "Take a drink for courage, sweetheart. Trust me, you're gonna need it."

"The ladies' room was occupied," I explained, observing the hungry inspection David gave Juliet. "We were just having a little bit of girl talk. Juliet was telling me about the night you two spent together."

I let one hand run along the outline of her nipple until I felt the hard bud begging to be sucked raw.

David laughed, but he appeared to be a bit embarrassed. "So she told you I was her first? We were in her parents' den, listening to a Billy Idol album. Hell, I still get excited every time I hear that song." The more he went on, the more my fingers stroked her nipple.

"Did you make her come?" I asked, tipping the booze up to her lips. "I mean, most girls don't get off the first time—but of course, Juliet isn't most girls."

He seemed to be having a rough time deciding where he should look—at my face or her body. "Hey, I didn't mean to cause any trouble between you," he said. "Christ, we were just kids."

I pulled out one of her small breasts; her legs were shaking and I had to tighten my grip to keep her from crumpling to the floor.

"Oh, don't stop, David," I said, watching Juliet's eyes pleading with me in the mirror behind him. She'd told me once that her first fuck was a college professor. "Christ, her nipples get hard as diamonds just thinking about it."

"I don't quite understand what's going on here, but I'm gonna leave you two alone," David said. But he was mesmerized and made no attempt to move.

"She wants to fuck you again," I said, pointing to the outer room. "Right there on the couch, just like old times."

I pushed Juliet's head down so that she was staring at his crotch. "Is that the effect you were wishing for, Princess?" The length of his cock was plainly visible through his pants.

"Cathy!" she cried. "I'm not..."

My fingers gripped like a vise, squeezing her nipple until her back stiffened. "Tell him how you said you wanted to relive losing your virginity--and this time, try not to lie. You know how much it disappoints me when you don't tell the truth."

I was hot again and David certainly appeared ready.

"Actually, we did it on the floor," he said, taking a few steps until he was close enough to touch her.

I set her breast free. "I told Juliet I wouldn't mind seeing your cock in her," I said. "If you're into it, that is."

I had his full attention. "You're not kidding, are you?" he said.

"Hey, if you don't want her, just walk away."

He moved slowly, unsure at first, bending to suck Juliet's hard pink nipple into his mouth. My arm held her tight as I rubbed against her ass. She struggled a bit but she couldn't stifle the moan that escaped her lips like a plea.

"Lets get comfortable, David." I passed him the bottle and led Juliet to the couch, pulling off cushions and tossing them to the floor in a makeshift bed.

"Cathy, please," she whispered, her lip quivering. "Forgive me. I shouldn't have made up that story about the guy in college. Okay?"

I bolted the lock on the door and stretched her out on her stomach like a sacrifice.

David finished off the champagne and followed us.

I jerked Juliet up on all fours, her head raised high enough to find forgiveness in my cunt, and pulled up my skirt. "I'm gonna watch him fuck you, Princess."

David knelt behind her sprawled legs, his suit pants open, the head of his cock twitching at her ass.

I bunched the dark red gown up at her back. "Spread out nice and wide for him, sweetie. Just like you did when you were in high school. Yes, that's a good girl. Now tell David what you want him to do. And thank me."

"Thank you, Cathy." Her breath was hot against my thighs and I knew she would come soon if I didn't hurry him up.

"Open me up like you did the first time, David," she said. "Hurry."

He stared at me as if afraid it might all be a misunderstanding.

I grabbed a handful of Juliet's hair, steadying her for the first thrust.

He grabbed her ass for leverage, driving his cock in so hard I could feel the force as her head was shoved into my cunt. Her mouth sucking me off turned my clit into another cock. This time she put her whole heart into the punishment. "You're my little slut, aren't you baby?" I asked through clenched teeth.

Juliet looked up at me and nodded her head, breathless. Suddenly she was moving with David, her backside pumping. I pulled her face back in to drink; her tongue snaked into my cunt. David worked her like a pro, pushing his cock in all the way and drawing it out again slowly. He reached down with one hand, stimulating her clit. Juliet cried out, wrapping her arms around my waist.

Each time he pulled back for the next careful plunge, I saw her juices on his slick cock. I was coming in her mouth, and I could feel building in her an orgasm so strong she couldn't control herself anymore.

Yanking Juliet's head back, I said, "He's about to fill that sweet little hole of yours. Come for me now."

She let go, crying out my name as I kissed her.

David groaned, his thrusts getting quicker and more forceful as an orgasm shook him.

I waited until he finished, then let Juliet slump like a rag doll at my feet. I ran my hand over her back. David zipped his pants and glanced around sheepishly, adjusting his hair and tie.

I better..." he said, pointing at the door. "Maryann's gonna be wondering what happened to me." With his hand on the doorknob he turned back, grinning like a schoolboy. "Christ, I hope like hell I'm not so drunk I forget this in the morning."

And he was gone.

Juliet smiled, kissing my face. "I have one more tiny confession to make."

"Oh no," I said, straightening her dress and pushing her breasts back into hiding. "Go ahead, out with it."

"Well, I kind of lost my virginity three times. David has two brothers and they're just as cute."

I laughed, wrapping my arms around her as we walked out into the hall. "You can point them out to me at the next family gathering."

What You're In For
Zonna

Den felt all the hairs stand up on the back of her neck, the way it is when you get a chill or when you know somebody's watching you. Seeing as it was the middle of July, she figured someone was checking her out. She didn't turn around right away, though. Had to be cool, make it seem casual, like she was bored. She waited a few minutes, working a rock loose with the toe of her sneaker and kicking it aimlessly along the fence.

This was one of the few institutions she'd been in where they still had dirt. Most seemed to cover it up with concrete soon as they could, denying you even that small amount of nature. It was like they didn't want you to come in contact with any living thing in these places, like that might give you hope or something. Hope was a dangerous thing in a prison. Hope makes a woman careless. Makes her forget. She might not take what they give so easy, thinking maybe she could change things. There'd be an end to look toward, instead of just doing what you have to, trying to make it through each day like it's all you're gonna get. Hope is words like *more*, or *better*. There ain't no room in lockup for words like that.

Sometimes, though, when no one was looking, Den would pretend to bend down to tie her shoe, and instead she'd run her fingers through that dirt and maybe put a little in her shirt pocket. That night in her cell, she'd lie there in the dark and smell it. It smelled like *tomorrow*; like *could be*. It smelled like hope.

When she did finally turn around, it was slow and easy like she didn't care, running a hand through her short blonde hair and squinting into the sun hanging over the prison wall. She took in the whole yard with one glance. Sure enough, that crazy bitch, Cole, was staring at her. Some girls called her Ice Cole 'cause her eyes were ice blue and she never showed no emotion on that stone-cold face of hers.

Den continued her stroll along the fence, away from Cole's scrutinizing gaze, ignoring the sweat that had started to trickle down her back. Cole was a menace. If Cole wanted to make things bad for Den, then they'd be bad.

Den was trying to do good time. She'd had more than enough hard time, in and out of institutions for one thing or another since she was fourteen. Twenty-seven was too old to have to be proving herself all over again. She didn't want any trouble. But if Cole started sniffing around, Den wasn't about to just roll over, belly-up. She'd have to be on alert; use those eyes she'd grown in the back of her head.

The whistle blew and they lined up. Den was careful to put a healthy number of bodies between Cole's and her own, but the other woman pushed through the line until she stood directly behind Den.

A finger traced a bead of sweat as it traveled from Den's hairline down her spine.

"You're mine." Cole's breath blew in Den's ear, making her shudder.

"Keep your fuckin' hands off me."

"We'll see," Cole chuckled under her breath.

"No talking." The guard tapped them both on the shoulders as she passed.

Cole took advantage of the moment to sneak her hand around and quickly pinch Den's nipple. She knew Den wouldn't protest with the guard so near.

Without thinking, Den stepped back, putting her heel down hard on Cole's foot. Immediately, the intruder's hand was gone.

"You're gonna be real sorry you did that," Cole hissed between clenched teeth.

Den stood up straighter as the line started moving forward.

"Real sorry," Cole promised.

"Someone's been aksin' 'bout you."

Den waited to hear if Beth was going to finish that thought or leave it dangling in the air. She'd learned not to appear too curious.

"Don't ya wanna know who?"

"Not particularly." Den figured she already knew.

"I bet if you knew who it was, you'd wanna know."

Den didn't even laugh anymore when her dumb-ass cell mate said stupid shit like that. She watched a hairy little spider finish spinning a web by the foot of her bed. Waited till it was almost finished, then destroyed the whole thing with one sweep of her hand. Almost immediately, the spider started over.

"It's Cole."

Den pretended she didn't care.

"She's sure been aksin' a lotta questions." Beth was dying to tell.

"Like?"

"Like, how long you in for, what you done to get here, where you was before, and like that."

"Who she been asking?"

"Just everyone," Beth rolled her eyes.

"Like you?"

"Maybe me."

Den rolled over onto her back and stared at the ceiling. She busied herself with a loose thread on the pocket of her shirt. She'd made a promise to herself that when she got out she'd never wear nothing blue again. Why'd they pick the color of sky, the color of freedom, to remind you that you weren't free? Some sick joke.

"I'll tell you what-all for a smoke," Beth said.

"Got none."

Den knew Beth would give it up sooner or later; she wasn't about to buy information she could get for free. Cigarettes were money; but time in a prison wasn't worth a damn. She could wait.

By lights out, Beth had told everything she knew, which wasn't really much.

Den lay awake for hours, her mind racing. Cole was definitely looking for trouble. And a woman like Cole usually found what she was looking for. In all the years she'd been behind bars, Den had never been nobody's property. Not like some hadn't tried to own her, big as she was. Seemed sometimes the bigger ones had more to worry about on the inside--so many wanted to cut you down. Bigger size, bigger prize. She'd managed to talk her way out of a lot of bad situations, but she'd learned way back in juvie that a quick right cross was just as valuable as a quick mind on this side of the wall. Her rep was pretty solid, just like she was. Even so, Den made a mental note to up her workout, just in case. A few more ounces of muscle behind her wouldn't hurt none.

"Go, girl... One more... That's it."

Den grunted as she lifted the barbell up and over, Tracy's

hands guiding but not touching, till the weight clicked back into place.

"Yeah! That was good." Tracy smiled in admiration. "You working toward something, or just working?"

Den sat up and rubbed the sweat into her muscles, kneading her sore arms, secretly enjoying the pain. Pain was a marker. If you could feel something, that meant you were still alive.

Tracy let her hands down easy onto Den's shoulders and started a slow massage, careful to keep it all business, even though she wished it was more. Den was hot—pumped, her muscles tight like she was carved out of solid rock. Tracy liked to be around her; to watch her lift, or run, or shoot hoops. Den was smooth, like water running down a hill. She had that certain grace you find in tall things, like giraffes or palm trees. When she moved, it was almost in slow motion. Tracy wished she could get closer to Den somehow. Wished she could move with her, feel Den's body rise and fall; wrap herself up in those strong arms.

"Den?"

"Mmm?"

"Why you working so hard today?"

"No reason," Den lied easily.

"Okay, if you say so. Seems to me you don't need to work so hard, though."

"No reason to get lazy."

Tracy tried to swallow the words in her throat before they fell out, but her mouth was too dry. "Den, I got something to say."

"So, say it."

"I'm scared you might get pissed off."

Den turned around to face Tracy, whose hands had dropped uselessly to her sides.

"I'll try not to get pissed. What is it?"

"I...I was wondering...I got feelings--"

"No fucking on the benches."

Cole's voice cut Tracy's sentence right in half.

Den stood up slowly, flexing her muscles, ready for trouble. Tracy all but disappeared in her shadow.

"You're looking real good, Denny." Cole flashed a greasy smile and reached out a hand to stroke Den's biceps.

Den shook her off.

"I told you before, don't be touching me, Cole."

"Why not?" Cole peered around Den's shoulder. Her frosty eyes zeroed in on Tracy. "Is this what you're turning me down for?"

Den ignored the question and started to walk away, bumping Cole's shoulder as she passed. A dangerous move, but a necessary one, Den decided.

Three steps later, a sound like "woof" made Den spin around. Tracy was doubled up on the ground. Two of Cole's girls stood nearby. Cole herself sat on the bench, shrugging her shoulders and shaking her head.

"Prison yard's a dangerous place. Never know what might happen. Best not to get too close to anybody." Cole checked the weights and started to lift where Den had left off.

Den hurried over to her friend. "You all right?" She helped Tracy to her feet.

"Yeah. I think so." Tracy brushed the dirt off her clothes.

"I'm sorry. That was about me, not you."

They started walking back toward the cells.

"You Cole's girl?" Tracy asked right out.

"Hell, no."

"But she wants you, right?"

"Yeah, well, I don't care much what she wants."

Tracy's knees got a little weak; she felt Den's arms holding her up.

"You sure you're all right?"

"I'm scared, Den."

"Don't be scared. I'll watch out for you. I promise. From now on, you just stick by me."

Tracy weighed the pain in her stomach against the words in her ear. She considered the scales even enough.

Den closed her eyes and turned her face up to the nozzle, felt the cool water splash over her, washing away the prison smell, if only for a few hours. It always returned, though: a strange mix of perspiration, desperation, and resignation. It got in your hair and under your skin. You could smell it on your own breath, and everyone else's. It was a part of the place, issued on the first day, along with your toothbrush and uniform. It was woven into the light blue fabric, tucked under the corner of every worn bed sheet. It was in the gravy, in the soap, pumped in through the air vents. There was no escaping it.

Suddenly, she felt rough hands pinning her arms behind her back and a bar of soap being shoved into her mouth. Her legs were pulled open by more hands. Her eyes snapped open.

"You sure are one hot-looking bitch."

Cole stood directly in front of her, wearing only her tattoos. She reached out a hand and ran it over Den's stomach.

"What's the matter? Nothing to say this time? Don't want me to stop?"

Den tried not to swallow and choke on the bitter soapsuds. She stood perfectly still. She knew she couldn't move and didn't want Cole to see her struggle.

"I see you're a natural blonde, Denny." Cole tangled her fingers in Den's pubic hair and gave it a yank. The four girls restraining her tightened their grip.

"Tell you what. We'll make it a fair game. Since you don't seem able to voice your opinions at the moment, I'll read your body language instead. If your nipples don't get hard, then I won't fuck you. Sounds, fair, don't it?"

Cole moved in closer and began licking the water from Den's breasts. Her tongue circled each nipple again and again; they rose like mountains from the sea.

"Well, well--looks like you been lying. Seems you want me to fuck you after all." Cole reached down between her captive's legs and--

Den woke up so hard she sat straight up. Her heart was pounding loud and fast, like the way the cops bang on your door in the middle of the night. She could still hear the shower running, still see the tiles all around her; still feel Cole's hands on her. She couldn't catch her breath. Sweat ran in her eyes and burned. She put her head between her knees and tried not to panic. Slowly, things started to wind back down to normal.

"What you doin'?" Beth's sleepy voice called from the lower bunk.

"Nothing."

"You sick or somethin'?"

"No. Go back to sleep."

"Don't puke in here. I hate that smell."

"I won't. Go to sleep."

Beth drifted off again, snoring softly.

Den stood up and tried to walk the dream off like a leg cramp. What was this about? A premonition? Some kind of warning? She didn't believe much in omens and such; didn't believe much in anything. Didn't make no sense to her that any kind of higher power would be bothering with someone in here. She knew Cole was after her ass. She didn't need a stupid dream to remind her.

So, what then? If it wasn't something she was supposed to watch out for, then what was it? Some people thought dreams were about things you wanted but couldn't say out loud, even to yourself. Well, she was damn sure she didn't want Cole raping her in no shower. *Damn* sure of that.

Maybe it was just about sex. Been years since she'd had any. Couldn't be healthy. Certainly not if it was giving her nightmares like this. Maybe it was time to get herself some-one. Plenty to choose from--Tracy, for one. Den could see herself with Tracy. And she knew Tracy was interested. She wouldn't suggest nothing serious or long-term; just for here and now. Maybe they could soften the time a little by sharing it. No harm in that.

Den chased her food around the plate but didn't swallow much. She was convinced most of it wasn't really made for swallowing. The bread was all right, if you liked stale bread. The vegetables were usually overcooked, though; boiled till the flavor evaporated along with any nutritional value they might have once had. And the meat seemed to be boiled, as well. You couldn't tell if it was supposed to be turkey, or beef, or ham. It was always sliced into the same thin, taste-less, pale gray strips. You could try to eat it like that, or you could hide it under a spoonful of lukewarm brown gravy. The choice was yours. The only time you knew for sure what you were eating was when they served hot dogs. Den thought that was pretty ironic.

She felt Tracy's leg rub against hers. It reminded her of what she'd decided.

"Sorry." Tracy shifted in her seat.

"You about finished?" Den stood up.

Tracy pushed her tray away. "Yeah. I can't eat any more of this."

"Come with me, then."

Tracy followed, thinking they were headed for the yard, until they walked right past the exit and kept on walking.

"Where we going, Den?"

"Someplace quiet."

"Library?" Tracy had seen Den read a book once. She

couldn't remember what it was about, but the cover had been a pretty shade of green.

Den continued down the corridor and turned the corner to the laundry room.

Tracy's feet stopped moving when she realized where they were going.

Den turned and took her hand. "Do you wanna go with me?"

"For real?" Tracy couldn't believe her wish was about to come true.

"Only if you want to." Den seemed almost shy, asking like that. Tracy stood up on her toes and kissed Den on the mouth.

Den had traded another inmate her next two days off to sneak them into the linen room for two hours. It was common practice, and most of the guards were usually willing to look the other way. The way they figured, if their charges were busy fucking, they wouldn't be fighting. And that suited them just fine.

As soon as the door closed behind them, Den set some sheets out on the linoleum floor. The only problem was the heat. The long, narrow room had no ventilation and the steam from the laundry slid in under the door. In the dim glow of a night-light you could almost see the droplets of water in the air.

Den sat down on the damp sheets and motioned for Tracy to join her. They had barely started to kiss when it became apparent they weren't alone. Whispers drifted over from the far corner, then silence; then a low moan. In the shadows, they could make out two bodies moving together. Tracy and Den smiled at one another and shrugged. Who ever heard of a private room in a prison anyway?

Tracy ran her hands up and down Den's arms, drawing her partner's attention back to their own corner.

"I've wanted to be with you for a long time, Denny."

"Oh, yeah?"

"I just didn't know if you wanted me, too."

"Sure I do."

Den began unbuttoning Tracy's shirt.

"Let me show you how much I want you. Sit back and watch me."

Den watched as Tracy stood and began to slowly strip away her uniform, swaying her hips real sexy-like, running her hands over her breasts the way she'd wanted Denny to do for months.

Maybe it was the close quarters or the heat, but Den started feeling kind of woozy. She was getting slick between her legs just watching Tracy's show and could hardly wait to get her hands on the girl. This was definitely something she needed. She was glad she'd had that crazy dream after all.

Just then she sensed a sudden movement from across the room. The shadow women were sitting up, watching Tracy's striptease with great interest. The taller one caught Den's eye and raised a finger to her lips as if to say, "Shhh. Don't do nothing to ruin the spell now."

Den, mesmerized by the dance and the steam and the want growing inside her, found herself even more turned-on by the thought of an audience. She rose to her knees and pulled Tracy's naked form to her, running her lips across the girl's stomach, till she felt Tracy's legs start to tremble. She stood then, scooped the girl up in her powerful arms and lowered her to the floor. Den kissed Tracy's mouth, their tongues tangling together like slippery snakes. She blazed a trail of kisses down Tracy's neck, across her shoulders, and took each nipple into her mouth, first one, then the other.

Tracy responded with soft sighs and shivers, reaching up to pull at Denny's shirt.

Den sat back and tugged it off over her head. As she did,

she got a clear look at her spectators. The shorter one she'd seen around, but didn't know her name. The tall one, though, was Cole. As soon as she realized who it was, Den felt her passion flare as if someone had poured gasoline on a barbecue. She stared into Cole's eyes and saw a sly smile creep across her face.

Cole motioned to Den with her hand, "Bring it on," like some kind of a challenge. Then she lay back against the wall, spread her legs wide, and pulled her partner's head toward her crotch. She stared right at Den and mouthed the words, "Fuck me."

Den lowered her body on top of Tracy's, their breasts rubbing together as they kissed. Her muscles rippled as she raised herself up and began grinding her thigh into Tracy's cunt, her eyes locked on Cole's.

"Oh, Denny," Tracy moaned, pulling Den's attention away from Cole, making her feel a slight pang of guilt.

"Yeah, baby. Feels good?" She gazed down at Tracy.

"Yessss."

Den couldn't keep her focus, though, and as soon as Tracy's eyes closed again, she found herself studying Cole; waiting for signs, as if Cole was the one she was doing. She kept up a steady pace, driving Tracy wild, determined to get to Cole through her. Sweat coated their bodies as Den brought Tracy closer and closer to the edge.

Tracy cried out and clawed at Den's back just as Cole's hips started to buck. The two women came together, filling the room with the sounds and smells of sex.

Den held Tracy close and rocked her back to earth, at the same time keeping one eye on Cole. She knew they weren't through yet. She knew what Cole wanted from her now.

Cole licked her lips and repositioned her partner, blocking herself from Den's view for a few moments while she did so.

Den let Tracy slip her shorts down; felt the cool of the

sheets against her skin, which was just about on fire. She leaned back against the wall so she would have a clear view across the room. She felt Tracy's lips on her breasts, then Tracy's fingers teasing her clit, sliding deliciously up and down and around. She still couldn't see what Cole was up to, though, and it made her wary.

"You're so wet." Tracy's voice drew Den's attention.

"Feels real good, baby, don't stop." Den held Tracy's head to her chest, urging her forward.

Cole had one of the only dildos in the whole lockup, which made her quite a popular girl. When she rose to her knees, Den could see the strap around her waist, and the heavy latex cock hanging down between her legs. She watched Cole stroke the length of it before sinking it into her girlfriend's pussy from behind with one hard shove. Cole grinned at Den as she slammed into her partner's cunt, each thrust a little deeper than the one before.

Den knew it was meant for her. Cole was fucking her, like she would have in the dream if Den hadn't woken up.

She whispered to Tracy, "Do me harder, baby--like that, yeah."

Tracy took the direction and her hand fucked Den harder, unconsciously matching Cole's strokes.

Den felt her cunt trying to swallow Tracy's hand; heard the *slurp slurp slurp* of her own juices. She fought the urge to close her eyes and give in to the feeling, concentrating instead on Cole's hips; imagining Cole pounding into her, tearing her apart, forcing her to face a desire so overwhelming she had no control over it. She knew she shouldn't want Cole to fuck her; she knew it was wrong, even as she lay there. Yet even if she'd wanted to stop, she couldn't. She was like a deep well with a bucket on a too-short string. She couldn't get enough. Sweat ran freely from every pore. She felt the climax coming, and for a minute she couldn't breathe. When she came, she let go with a groan that grew from the back of her throat like a growl. Her body spasmed as she watched a satisfied smile split Cole's face in two.

Tracy looked up at Den, damn proud of herself—until she saw the truth in Denny's eyes. Busted. Then she just got real quiet, put her clothes on without a word, and went back to her cell.

That night, Den lay in her bed, reliving it all. Like a scene from a movie she didn't understand, she played it over and over in her mind, trying to figure out where she'd lost the thread. She didn't want Cole, did she? She'd wanted to be with Tracy. So why had she been so turned-on by Cole's game? Why hadn't she been able to stop it, to get up and leave? It was as if she was chained and shackled by the lust Cole had drawn to the surface. Had it always been there? Den closed her eyes and drifted off to a troubled sleep, doubting everything she'd ever known.

It doesn't matter what you're in for. It doesn't matter how guilty or innocent you think you are. There're prisons on either side of the wall.

Excerpt from *Portrait in Sepia*
Isabel Allende

Jealousy. The person who hasn't felt it cannot know how much it hurts, or imagine the madness committed in its name. In my thirty years I have suffered it only once, but I was burned so brutally that I have scars that still haven't healed, and I hope never will, as a reminder to avoid that feeling in the future. Diego wasn't mine—no person can belong to another—and the fact that I was his wife gave me no right over him or his feelings; love is a free contract that begins with a spark and can end the same way. A thousand dangers threaten love, but if the couple defends it, it can be saved; it can grow like a tree and give shade and fruit, but that happens only when both partners participate. Diego never did; our relationship was damned from the start. I realize that today, but then I was blind, at first with pure rage and later with grief.

Spying on him, watch in hand, I began to be aware that my husband's absences did not coincide with his explanations. When supposedly he had gone out hunting with Eduardo, he would come back hours earlier or later than his brother; when the other men in the family were at the sawmill or at the roundup branding cattle, he would suddenly show up in the patio, and later, if I raised the subject at the table, I would find that he hadn't been with them at any time during the day. When he went to town for supplies he would come back without anything presumably because he hadn't found what he was looking for, although it might be something as common as an ax or a saw. In the countless hours the family spent together, he avoided conversation at all cost; he was always the one who organized the card games or asked Susana to sing. If she came down with one of her headaches, he was quickly bored and would go off on his horse with his shotgun over his shoulder. I couldn't follow him on horseback without his seeing me or raising suspicion in the family, but I could keep an eye on him when he was around the house. That was how I noticed that sometimes he got up in the middle of the night, and that he didn't go to the kitchen to get something to eat, as I had always thought, but dressed, went out to the patio, disappeared for an hour or two, then quietly slipped back to bed. Following him in the darkness was easier than during the day, when a dozen eyes were watching us; it was all a matter of staying awake and avoiding wine at dinner and the bedtime opium drops.

One night in mid-May I noticed when he slipped out of bed, and in the pale light of the oil lamp we always kept lit before the cross, I watched him put on his pants and boots, pick up his shirt and jacket, and leave the room. I waited a few instants, then quickly got out of bed and followed him, with my heart about to burst out of my breast. I couldn't see him very well in the shadows of the house, but when he went out on the patio his silhouette stood out sharply in the light of the full moon, which for moments at a time shone bright in the heavens. The sky was streaked with clouds that cloaked everything in darkness when they hid the moon. I heard the dogs bark and was afraid they would come to me and betray my presence, but they didn't; then I understood that Diego had tied them up earlier.

My husband made a complete circle of the house and then walked rapidly toward one of the stables where the family's personal mounts were kept, the ones not used in the fields; he swung the crossbar that fastened the door and went inside. I stood waiting, protected by the blackness of an elm a few yards from the barn, barefoot and wearing nothing but a thin nightgown, not daring to take another step, convinced that Diego would come out on horseback, and I wouldn't be able to follow him. I waited for a period that seemed very long, but nothing happened.

Suddenly I glimpsed a light through the slit of the open door, maybe a candle or small lantern. My teeth were chattering, and I was shivering from cold and fright. I was about to give up and go back to bed when I saw another figure approaching from the east—obviously not from the big house—and also go into the stable, closing the door behind. I let almost fifteen minutes go by before I made a decision, then forced myself to take a few steps. I was stiff from the cold and barely able to move. I crept toward the door, terrified, unable to imagine how Diego would react if he found me spying on him, but incapable of retreating. Softly I pushed the door, which opened without resistance because the bar was on the outside and it couldn't be secured from the inside, and slipped like a thief through the narrow opening. It was dark in the stable, but a pale light flickered far at the back, and I tiptoed in that direction, almost not breathing—unnecessary precautions since the straw deadened my footsteps and several of the horses were awake; I could hear them shifting and snuffling in their stalls.

In the faint light of a lantern hanging from a beam and swayed by the wind filtering between the wooden timbers, I saw them. They had spread blankets out in a clump of hay, like a nest, where she was lying on her back, dressed in a heavy, unbuttoned overcoat under which she was naked. Her arms and her legs were spread open, her head tilted toward her shoulder, her black hair covering her face, and her skin shining like blond wood in the delicate, orangeish glow of the lantern.

Diego, wearing nothing but his shirt, was kneeling before her, licking her sex. There was such absolute abandon in Susana's position and such contained passion in Diego's actions that I understood in an instant how irrelevant I was to all that. In truth, I didn't exist, nor did Eduardo or the three children, no one else, only the two of them and the inevitability of their lovemaking. My husband had never caressed me in that way. It was easy to see that they had been like this a thousand times before, that they had loved each other for years; I understood finally that Diego had married me because he needed a screen to hide his love affair with Susana. In one instant the pieces of that painful jigsaw puzzle fell into place; I could explain his indifference to me, the absences that coincided with Susana's headaches, Diego's' tense relationship with his brother Eduardo, the deceit in his behavior toward the rest of the family, and how he arranged always to be near her, touching her, his foot against hers, his hand on her elbow or her shoulder, and sometimes, as if coincidentally, at her waist or her neck, unmistakable signs the photographs had revealed to me. I remembered how much Diego loved her children, and I speculated that maybe they weren't his nephews but his sons, all three with blue eyes, the mark of the Domînguezes. I stood motionless, gradually turning to ice as voluptuously they made love, savoring every stroke, every moan, unhurried, as if they had all the rest of their lives. They did not seem like a couple of lovers in a hasty clandestine meeting but like a pair of newlyweds in the second week of their honeymoon, when passion is still intact, but with added confidence and the mutual knowledge of each other's flesh. I, nevertheless, had never experienced intimacy of that kind with my husband, nor would I have been able to invent it in my most audacious fantasies. Diego's tongue was running over Susana's inner thighs, from her ankles upward, pausing between her legs and then back down again, while his hands moved from her waist to her round, opulent breasts, playing with her nipples, hard and lustrous as grapes. Susana's soft, smooth body shivered and undulated; she was a fish in the river, her head turning from side to side in the desperation of her pleasure, her hair spread across her face, her lips open in a long moan, her hands seeking Diego to guide him over the beautiful topography of her body, until his tongue made her explode in pleasure. Susana arched backward from the ecstasy that shot through her like lightning, and she uttered a hoarse cry that he choked off with his mouth upon hers. Then Diego took her in his arms, rocking her, petting her like a cat, whispering a rosary of secret words into her ear with a delicacy and tenderness I never thought possible in him. At some moment she sat up in the straw, took off her coat, and began to kiss him, first his forehead, then his eyelids, his temples, lingering on his mouth; her tongue mischievously explored Diego's ears, swerved to his Adam's apple, brushed across his throat, her teeth nibbling his nipples, her fingers combing the hair on his chest. Then it was his turn to abandon himself completely to her caresses; he lay face down on the blanket and she sat astride him, biting the nape of his neck, covering his shoulders with brief playful kisses, moving down to his buttocks, exploring, smelling, savoring him, and leaving a trail of saliva as she went. Diego turned over, and her mouth enveloped his erect, pulsing penis in an interminable labor of pleasure, of give and take in the most profound intimacy conceivable, until he could not wait any longer and threw himself on her, penetrated her, and they rolled like enemies in a tangle of arms and legs and kisses and panting and sighs and expressions of love that I had never heard before. Then they dozed in a warm embrace, covered with blankets and Susana's overcoat like a pair of innocent children. Silently I retreated and went back to the house, while the icy cold of the night poured inexorably through my soul.

A chasm opened before me; I felt vertigo pulling me downward, a temptation to leap and annihilate myself in the depths of suffering and fear. Diego's betrayal and my dread of the future left me floating with nothing to cling to, lost, disconsolate. The fury that had shaken me at first lasted only briefly, then I was crushed by a sensation of death, of absolute agony. I had entrusted my life to Diego, he had promised me his protection as a husband; I believed literally the ritual words of marriage: that we were joined until death us did part. There was no way out. The scene in the stable had confronted me with a reality that I had perceived for a long time but had refused to face.

My first impulse was to run to the big house, to stand in the middle of the patio and howl like a madwoman, to wake the family, the servants, the dogs, and make them witnesses to adultery and incest. My timidity, however, was stronger than my desperation. Silently, feeling my way in the dark, I dragged myself back to the room I shared with Diego and sat in my bed shivering and sobbing, my tears soaking into the neck of my nightgown. In the following minutes or hours I had time to think about what I had seen and to accept my powerlessness. It wasn't a sexual affair that joined Diego and Susana, it was a proven love; they were prepared to run every risk and sweep aside any obstacle that stood in their way, rolling onward like an uncontainable river of molten lava. Neither Eduardo nor I counted; we were disposable, barely insects in the enormity of their passion.

I should tell my brother-in-law before anyone else, I

decided, but when I pictured the blow such a confession would be to that good man, I knew I wouldn't have the courage to do it. Eduardo would discover it himself some day, or with luck, he might never know. Perhaps he suspected, as I did, but didn't want to confirm it in order to maintain the fragile equilibrium of his illusions; he had the three children, his love for Susana, and the monolithic cohesion of his clan.

Diego came back some time during the night, shortly before dawn. By the light of the oil lamp he saw me sitting on my bed, my face puffy from crying, unable to speak, and he thought I had woken with another of my nightmares. He sat beside me and tried to draw me to his chest, as he had on similar occasions, but instinctively I pulled away from him, and I must have worn an expression of terrible anger, because immediately he moved back to his own bed. We sat looking at each other, he surprised and I despising him, until the truth took form between the two of us, as undeniable and conclusive as a dragon.

"What are we going to do now?" were the only words I could utter.

He didn't try to deny anything or justify himself; he defied me wth a steely stare, ready to defend his love in any way necessary, even if he had to kill me. Then the dam of pride, good breeding, and politeness that had held me back during months of frustration collapsed, and silent reproaches were converted into a flood of recriminations that I couldn't contain, that he listened to quietly and without emotion, attentive to every word. I accused him of everything that had gone through my mind and then begged him to reconsider; I told him that I was willing to forgive and forget, that we could go far away somewhere no one knew us, and start over.

By the time my words and tears were exhausted, it was broad daylight. Diego crossed the distance that separated our beds, sat beside me, took my hands, and calmly and seriously explained that he had loved Susana for many years, and that their love was the most important thing in his life, more compelling than honor, than the other members of his family, than the salvation of his very soul. To make me feel better, he said, he could promise that he would give her up, but it would be an empty promise. He added that he had tried to do that when he went to Europe, leaving her behind for six months, but it hadn't worked. Then he had gone so far as to marry me, to see whether in that way he might break that terrible tie to his sister-in-law, but far from helping him in the decision to leave her, marriage had made it easier because it diluted the suspicions of Eduardo and the rest of the family. He was, however, happy that finally I had discovered the truth because it was painful to him to deceive me. He had nothing to say against me, he assured me. I was a good wife, and he deeply regretted that he couldn't give me the love I deserved. He felt miserable every time he slipped away from me to be with Susana; it would be a relief not to lie to me anymore. Everything was in the open now.

"And Eduardo doesn't count?" I asked.

"What happens between him and Susana is up to them. It's the relation between you and me that we must decide now."

"You have already decided, Diego. I don't have anything to do here, I will go back home," I told him.

"This is your house now, we are husband and wife, Aurora. What God has joined together you cannot put asunder."

"You are the one who has violated holy commandments," I pointed out.

"We can live together like brother and sister. You won't want for anything. I will always respect you, you will be protected and free to devote yourself to your photographs, or whatever you want. The only thing I ask is, please do not create a scandal."

"You can't ask anything of me, Diego."

"I'm not asking for myself. I have thick skin, and I can face it like a man. I'm asking for my mother's sake. She couldn't bear it."

So for Doña Elvira's sake, I stayed...

I was willing to stay at Caleufu, hiding my humiliation as a rejected wife, because if I left and she discovered the truth she would die of grief and shame. Her life turned around that family, around the needs of each of the persons who lived within the walls of their compound: that was her entire universe. My agreement with Diego was that I would play my part as long as Doña Elvira lived, and after that I would be free; he would let me leave and would never contact me again. I would have to live with the stigma—calamitous for many—of being "separated," and would not be able to marry again, but at least I wouldn't have to live with a man who didn't love me.

Translated by Margaret Sayers Peden

Am I Naked Yet?

Jane Underwood

"Can I join you?" Joel says to me one afternoon just as I am about to take a bath. "Would you like that?"

He has appeared on my threshold as if out of nowhere, which he often does. It's a Sunday, and I have just bid the computer repairman good-bye after his fourth emergency house call of the week. The good news is that he has finally managed to retrieve most of the corrupted files. The bad news is, my brain feels like it's been sizzling in oil.

"God, I'm fried after all this computer crap," I say. "Yes, I would love it if you would join me. I really need to relax."

What I refrain from mentioning is that I am also exhausted due to the hot flashes and night sweats that kept me from getting a decent night's sleep.

The water has risen almost to the top of my old claw foot tub, and the amber sunlight twirls in pirouettes across my dreamy liquid oasis.

"Then my timing couldn't be more perfect," says Joel. "Why don't you take off your clothes, get into the water, and let me bathe you. I'd like to run my soapy hands all over your body and wash you the way I'd wash a little child." The pitch of his voice drops two octaves lower as he moves into that muted, secretive tone that always makes me feel like we're the only lovers in the world. "Would you like me to kneel beside you, with all my clothes still on, and give you a long, luxurious bath?" he asks.

Like a startled school of minnows, my desire begins to dart to and fro.

"Uh huh," I say. "I'm really glad you're here."

"Good. You have such beautiful arms, such a beautiful neck. I want to wash every inch of you. Will you let me do that? Will you close your eyes and let me bathe you?"

"Yes," I say again, feeling, as I always do with Joel, as if I'm being guided into an erotic trance.

We first met through an Internet personals ad. Our emails soon led to a phone call that left me trembling and melting at my kitchen table. After that, we quickly became sexual. At this point, he has already fucked me in the bedroom, the office and the kitchen--but this is the first time I've invited him into my bath.

He waits as I pull my cotton T-shirt up over my head and step out of my jeans and panties. I can feel his intense gold-flecked hazel eyes taking me in. He has already told me how much he loves the freckles on my arms, and that my pale Irish skin turns him on. I take three steps to the tub, lift my leg over the egg-smooth curve of porcelain and, as my toes dip down past the surface, wonder if he notices the tinkling overture of water. I want him to hear this splash of song. I want him to hear what I hear, smell what I smell, touch what I touch.

I wonder, too, how the cleft in his beard-stubbled chin might taste today--maybe, I think, like the crusty, salty rim of a margarita glass. But more than his taste, I crave the hypnotic sound of his voice. When his words take on that whispery, rhythmical tone, he can talk me right over the edge of the highest cliff. His words are almost like a chant: "I won't stop. Don't worry. I like it. I won't stop, I won't stop, I won't stop. You can have as much as you want, sweetheart. I won't stop. I like it, I like it."

I lift the phone from the tile counter, raise it back up to my ear and say, "Are you still there?" He lives a country away, and I know we will never meet in person--never compare the images we've seen of each other on the screen to the actual, flesh and blood human beings. Not that it really matters. We have been lovers for over a year, and each time we're together, it only gets better.

"I'm here," Joel says. "Are you naked yet?"

I look at my reflection in the mirror. The ripples blur my face nicely, disguising the years as I sink lower, submerging my shoulders. Bobbing like two life buoys, my nipples are the only part of me that remain unobscured.

"Yes," I whisper to the young man, who at times reminds me of my own son. "I am."

About The Authors

ISABEL ALLENDE was born in Peru and raised in Chile. She is the author of the novels *Portrait in Sepia, Daughter of Fortune, The Infinite Plan, Eva Luna, Of Love and Shadows,* and *The House of the Spirits*; the short story collection *The Stories of Eva Luna*; the memoir *Paula*; and *Aphrodite: A Memoir of the Senses.* She lives in California.

BETTY BLUE is a bratty bi chick with a taste for fine porn. Betty's fiction has appeared in *Best Bisexual Erotica, Anything That Moves, Tough Girls, Best Lesbian Erotica 2002,* and *Best Lesbian Love Stories.*

CHEYENNE BLUE'S stories have appeared online at www.cleansheets.com and www.brilliantsmut.com. Her story "Shadow Child" was included in *Best Women's Erotica 2001.*

CARA BRUCE is the editor of *Best Fetish Erotica, Best Bisexual Women's Erotica,* and *Viscera.* She is coauthor of *The First Year--Hepatitis C.* Her short fiction has been published in tons of anthologies including *Best Women's Erotica*, *Best American Erotica*, *Best Lesbian Erotica*, *Mammoth Book of Best New Erotica* and many more. Her fiction and nonfiction has appeared in magazines, newspapers and websites, including Salon.com, *San Francisco Bay Guardian* and *While You Were Sleeping*. She is the founder/editor/publisher of www.venusorvixen.com and Venus or Vixen Press.

RACHEL KRAMER BUSSEL's writing has appeared in the *San Francisco Chronicle, Bust, Curve, On Our Backs, Playgirl*, and several anthologies including *Best Lesbian Erotica 2001, Starf*cker, Faster Pussycats*, and *Tough Girls*. She is coauthor of *The Erotic Writer's Market Guide*. Visit her at www.rachelkramerbussel.com.

ANN DULANEY lives and writes in Copenhagen, Denmark. Her work has been published in www.cleansheets.com, *Mind Caviar, Erotic Travel Tales* and *Best Lesbian Erotica 2002*. Feel free to contact her at anndulaney@yahoo.com.

CLIO KNIGHT lives in Hobart, a small city at the foot of a mountain in the luscious green island state of Tasmania. Her work has been published in various webzines including www.*amoretonline.com, www.seska4lovers.com, and www.amatory-ink.co.uk*. "Strawberry Surprise" was her first published erotic story, originally appearing in *Australian Women's Forum*.

EDEN LENZ is cofounder of a writing website and editor of an electronic journal. She has one husband and one dog. Her most passionate interests are writing, sex, and pissing people off.

DAWN O'HARA'S stories appear in *Ripe Fruit: Erotica for Well-Seasoned Lovers, Shameless: Women's Intimate Erotica*, and, under other names, in *Calyx* and *Mind Caviar*. She was a Hedgebrook resident, contest winner for the Seattle Writers Association and Redmond Spoken Word Association, and a finalist for the Silver Clitoride Best Story of the Month. Contact her at dawno_hara@hotmail.com.

CELIA O'TOOLE lives in the San Francisco Bay Area with her husband and two school-aged children. While writing erotica is one of her favorite pastimes, she usually writes non-fiction, focusing on personal effectiveness, parenting, and relationships. She has authored one book along with numerous articles and essays.

LISA PROSIMO lives in the wine country of California with her husband. When she's not writing, she spends her time gazing out her window at all those grapes.

SAIRA RAMASASTRY was an English-Speaking Union Scholar to Cambridge University where she received her M.Phil.; she received her M.S. and B.A. from Stanford. Her stories have appeared or will appear in *Scifidimensions*, *Rosebud* and *ZYZZYVA*.

JEAN ROBERTA writes articles and reviews for queer and erotic journals as well as erotic stories, which have appeared in the *Best Lesbian Erotica* series, a previous volume of *Best Women's Erotica*, and numerous other anthologies including *Ripe Fruit: Erotica for Well-Seasoned Lovers* and *Shameless: Women's Intimate Erotica*. Her e-novel, *Prairie Gothic*, is in the catalog of Amatory Ink (www.amatory-ink.co.uk).

BARBARA RODUNER writes because it's the first thing she thinks of in the morning after she's dreamed about it all night. Her real world is inside her mind, where she entertains any number of weird notions—a world that only flourishes because of her family's loving support. *Molto grazie*, Larry!

RACHEL RESNICK is the author of the novel *Go West Young F*cked Up Chick* and a contributing editor at *Tin House* magazine. She has had fiction, plays, and nonfiction published in the *Los Angeles Times, Tin House, The Ohio Review, Chelsea, Absolute Disaster: Fiction from LA, LA Shorts,* and *Best Bisexual Women's Erotica,* among others. She lives in Topanga Canyon with her scarlet macaw, Ajax. Visit her Web site: www.rachelresnick.com.

MICHELLE SCALISE has sold over two hundred poems and short stories to such anthologies as *Wicked Words 6, Best Bisexual Women's Erotica, Best Women's Erotica 2001, Dark Arts, The Darker Side, Viscera, Darkness Rising, Bell Book & Beyond,* and *The Urbanite.*

CECILIA TAN is the author of *Black Feathers, The Velderet,* and *Telepaths Don't Need Safewords.* Her erotic short stories have appeared everywhere from *Penthouse* to *Ms., Asimov's Science Fiction* to *Best American Erotica.* She writes about her passions (sex, baseball, and food) from Cambridge, Massachusetts. Her Web site: www.ceciliatan.com

ALISON TYLER has penned sixteen naughty novels, including *Strictly Confidential, Sweet Thing,* and *Sticky Fingers,* all published by Black Lace. Her short stories have appeared in *Best Women's Erotica 2002, Erotic Travel Tales, Guilty Pleasures, Wicked Words 4, 5, and 6* and *Sweet Life.*

JANE UNDERWOOD'S erotica has appeared in periodicals, such as *Libido* and *Yellow Silk,* and anthologies, such as *The Ecstatic Moment,* and *Ripe Fruit.* She is also a poet, personal essayist, teacher, entrepreneur and mother of an amazing, circus-performing son. She lives in San Francisco where she runs The Writing Salon, a school of creative writing.

ZONNA is old enough to be Britney Spear's mother. (And the less said about that, the better.) You may have seen her short stories in anthologies from Alyson Publications, Arsenal Pulp Press, Seal Press, Odd Girls Press, or Black Books.

About the Editor

MARCY SHEINER, editor of the *Best Women's Erotica* series and *The Oy of Sex: Jewish Women's Erotica* (Cleis Press), has edited ten collections of women's erotica and still isn't tired of it. Her how-to, *Sex for the Clueless*, was published by Kensington. *Perfectly Normal*, her memoir of raising a child with a disability, is available at iUniverse.com, as well as at Amazon.com and Barnes&Noble.com. Visit her at http://marcysheiner.tripod.com.